MW01517853

SECRETS IN
O'HALLERAN BAY

AN *Arvilla Badger* MYSTERY

S. HEWITT

To my family, all of whom are great storytellers. To my daughters, who have always appreciated a good story and have the makings of excellent storytellers.

Contents

Prologue

The war gave us all secrets.

I kept mine longer than I needed to; I see that now. Here I am, more than half a century later, and everyone I was keeping those secrets from is either dead or curled up in a hospital bed wearing diapers. It's a terrible, lonely feeling to be one of the last ones at the end. At my age, I can't really expect too many more years above ground so maybe that's why I finally decided to tell my stories to you and let go of some of those secrets. Or, (and this explanation is really more likely if I'm being honest) maybe I'm just horribly vain and want people to see me as something other than a stooped, white-haired little old lady in elastic waist pants and ugly shoes. It would be nice for people to look at me in awe, shake their heads and mutter, "Boy! Wasn't she something!".

The first secret I kept, and certainly the one I am most ashamed of, was that I didn't hate the war. I didn't even dislike it. Don't be an idiot; of course I hated the death and the suffering that happened because of it. I hated that people willingly turned against each other and performed the basest, most unfathomable acts on fellow human beings. I hated the death of the innocent. But I could never make myself hate the war itself. Since I'm being truthful here, I will tell you that I loved it, which probably means I'm sick in the head.

It was the thought of returning home that I both hated and feared. For four years I had been trusted with authority and responsibility. I'd lived as an independent woman, doing as I pleased (and with whomever I pleased) without judgement. The war showed me exactly what I was capable of and who I could be. But the world I was returning to had already planned the rest of my life for me: I would find a suitable man and get married, pop out children and spend the rest of my life sewing costumes for school plays and testing out new recipes for meatloaf. These things, which had once been so important to me, no longer interested me in the least by the spring of 1945 when I returned home from Europe and I was determined to avoid the man-marriage-baby route other girls my age were taking. I suppose this is the reason I jumped at the chance to work for the O'Halleran Bay Police Force. Not as an officer, of course. In those days there were no female police officers. No, I was hired to answer phones, file papers, take messages and make coffee.

The second secret I kept, which was never much of a secret to anyone who watched me work a typewriter, was that I did not spend the war as a typist at Army Headquarters.

One

MAY 1946

I was awakened by a sharp and steady thud that I, at first, mistook for a raging headache caused by too many drinks, not enough food and going to sleep well past dawn. As I lay staring up at the ceiling, cursing myself for my stupidity and promising never to drink so much and stay out so late again (vows I'd made hundreds of times before, I'm afraid), I gradually came to realize that the noise was actually the sound of someone knocking loudly and repeatedly on the wooden screen door at the front of the cottage. I groaned and rolled over, covered my head with the quilt and tried to block out the sun that streamed into the little yellow bedroom. As far as I was concerned, whoever was knocking could blow it out his ass. The knocking continued, growing louder and more insistent. Daylight slipped through the worn fabric of the bed covers. Incensed, I rolled out of bed and stumbled through the large living room to the kitchen, slightly disoriented by my surroundings. I squinted, trying to shut out some of the day's brightness, fumbling for the knob on the front door until I grasped it and wrenched open the door angrily.

A young man wearing a navy blue tunic bearing the emblem of the O'Halleran Bay Police Force looked up at me, slightly surprised. He took off his peaked cap and tucked it under his arm. "Miss Badger? Miss Arvilla Badger?"

"Yes," I croaked, taking a step forward and opening the screen door.

"Corporal Joe McKay, O'Halleran Bay Police Force. I'm sorry to bother you, miss, but I need to speak with you."

I froze, suddenly alert. "Is it my brother? Did something happen to Johnny?"

"No. It's nothing like that." He gestured with his cap to my slip, which I hadn't thought to cover with a robe before opening the door. "Perhaps you'd care to get dressed first?" he asked, slightly embarrassed but more amused.

I nodded. "I'll just be a few minutes."

My dress lay on the kitchen floor where I'd left it only a few hours before. It was wrinkled and more appropriate for an evening of cocktails than a Saturday morning at a cottage in rural Ontario but the rest of my clothes were still packed in suitcases in the car. After dressing, I raked my fingers through my hair and hastily pinned one side up with a bobby pin. Declaring myself presentable, I unlocked the kitchen door and the police officer, his lanky frame leaning against the porch railing, hastily stood. "Please, come inside Constable," I said, holding open the wooden screen door.

He bent down and picked up a bottle of milk from the porch. "It's Corporal," he corrected me, stepping inside the cottage and handing me the milk. "Corporal McKay."

"You'll have to excuse me. I didn't leave Toronto until after midnight and it was a slow drive up here in the dark. I got to bed just as the sun came up." I gestured to a chair at the kitchen table and set the milk down on the kitchen counter.

McKay sat down and took a small leather notebook out of his breast pocket. "I apologize for waking you."

I opened one of the kitchen cupboards and glanced at its contents. "I'm afraid I don't have any tea but can I offer you some coffee? I developed quite a taste for it while I was overseas. The Americans love their coffee."

"Nothing for me, thank you. Ed Haggerty told me you were in England. CWAC, right?" he asked.

I smiled. Ed had looked after my family's cottage for decades and could always be counted on to know everybody's business. "I was trained in wireless operation in Québec at Sainte-Anne-de-Bellevue and in '42 I was sent to the War Office in London." My reply, the one I'd rehearsed a thousand times, was short and to the point, boring and unlikely to elicit further questions or require additional details. I filled the percolator with water, set it on the electric stove and turned on the burner. "You?"

"Canadian Provost Corps."

"Military police. You were in Europe, then?"

He nodded. "France, Italy and then Holland."

I grabbed the pack of Export cigarettes from the table and tapped one out, looking around for the matches I knew I'd had the night before. No luck. "Holland. That must have been rough."

"Winter of '45 was the worst."

I shuddered and involuntarily rubbed my arms even though the late May weather gave the cottage a warm and comforting air. "I saw the pictures."

Giving up on the matches, I turned on the large stove burner. It glowed bright orange within seconds and I leaned down and lit my cigarette, inhaling deeply. I exhaled and nodded towards the cigarette. "Another habit I picked up overseas."

"Those things will kill you," McKay said.

"A lot of things will kill you," I answered.

"Another habit you picked up from those damn Americans?" McKay smiled.

"The Americans might be to blame for the coffee and the alcohol but the Scots are at fault for the cigarettes."

"Funny. I would have thought it would be the other way around," he quipped. "And what are the Canadians at fault for?"

I exhaled slowly. "That's a story for another time, Corporal. Maybe when we know each other a little bit better."

McKay reddened slightly and glanced down at his notebook, pretending to check something he'd written. "I've come to ask you a few questions, Miss Badger. The O'Halleran Bay Police Force is investigating the possible disappearance of a man who rented this cottage in 1941 for the month of July."

I sat back in my chair. "A disappearance? Here? In 1941?" I said finally.

"It's a possible disappearance," McKay repeated. "We're trying to determine whether the man

is missing of his own accord or has genuinely disappeared. The man we're looking for went missing
sometime between July 18th and 23rd, 1941."

"I'm afraid I won't be any help. I can't even remember if I came up to the cottage that summer.
It may sound silly but it feels like 1941was in the
distant past, a whole lifetime ago." I shook my head
and tapped the ashes from my cigarette into the
ashtray on the table.

He nodded. "I know what you mean."

"My father might have been able to tell you something but he died last October."

"I know. I was sorry to hear about his death,"
McKay said.

"Did you know him?"

"Not well. My father owns McKay Drugs here in
town. Doc Badger and my old man used to sit at the
counter and complain about the Maple Leafs but it
had been years since I'd last talked to him. He was
a surgeon at a big Toronto hospital, wasn't he?"

"Yes. Toronto Western. After he retired he decided to spend most of his time here in O'Halleran
Bay."

"Ed Haggerty told me your father kept a notebook with records about his renters; names, dates,
payments, notes, that sort of thing. That's why
I'm here. I was hoping I could take a look at your

9

father's notebooks for the summer of 1941. He may have noticed something that could be helpful to this investigation."

"Of course," I set my cigarette down in the ashtray. "I assume all of his notebooks are in his office upstairs but honestly, everything is in complete disarray right now. I'll turn them over to you as soon as I can find them. In the meantime, you might also check with Cedar Lake Lodge. Father told me that often the Lodge sent people his way if they were booked up. They might have some more information."

He took a photograph from the back of his notebook and slid it across the table. "Do you know this man?"

I picked it up and examined the face of the attractive blond man staring confidently at the photographer's lens. "Is this the man who's missing?"

"Yes. You both went to the University of Toronto and graduated the same year. He was at Osgoode."

I smiled and handed him back the photograph. "There are thousands of students at U of T and there were hundreds of graduates that year. He was studying to become a lawyer; I was perfecting my Italian and French in the Modern Languages programme. I doubt our paths would have crossed."

"His name is Hugh Adams."

I shook my head. "His name doesn't sound familiar either but as I said, it's unlikely we would have crossed paths. I can't imagine the O'Halleran Bay Police Force is so busy that it's taken this long to get around to investigating a disappearance that happened five years ago."

"I can't talk about that. It's private information," McKay said.

"Come now, Corporal. If it's information I could hear down at Hudson's Lunch Counter then I doubt very much it's private," I said.

McKay smirked and set down his pencil. "Adam's family assumed that he had run off and joined up. When he didn't reappear after the war, his sister contacted the War Office. She was worried he'd been killed overseas and they hadn't been advised. The War Office has no record that he ever enlisted. That's why we're looking into this matter now. It's just routine, really. I'm sure he'll turn up."

"Did anyone contact the C Int C?" I asked.

"The Canadian Intelligence Corps? Why?"

"He sounds exactly like the type of man they'd recruit. Educated, handsome, clever, sly, a risk-taker. Someone who could exist quite comfortably in a morally grey area."

McKay sat back in his chair. "You got all of that from looking at his picture?"

I picked up my cigarette, drew in and exhaled a small cloud of smoke. "I got all of that from the fact that he was a lawyer."

He smiled a lopsided grin, revealing a dimple on his left cheek. "Wouldn't the War Office have that information?"

"It depends on who you ask at the War Office. If Adams was working for the C Int C, his file may not be available to just anybody. He could still be working for them. The U.S. and Great Britain don't trust the Russians." At his quizzical look, I smiled and shrugged. "The things you learn working at military headquarters."

"I'll have my Chief look into it." McKay jotted down more notes in his notebook.

I stubbed my cigarette out in the ashtray as McKay stood to leave. "I suppose you've searched the most obvious spot." I gestured out the large kitchen window to the lake.

He looked out and across the lawn to the quiet water that stretched out like a piece of perfect, unblemished glass that morning. "Cedar Lake doesn't keep a secret very well. It's only ten miles long and barely three miles across. Some spots reach thirty feet deep but most of it's under twenty feet. Why, you probably have to walk twenty or thirty feet from the beach out there before the water goes over your head. There are six islands and countless sandbars. Just ask any of the old-timers around town; bodies always float to the surface and wash up on a beach somewhere." McKay ran a hand through his light brown hair and set his cap back on his head. "Thank you for your offer of coffee but I have to be getting back to the station."

I accompanied him to the door. "I'll get Father's notebooks to you as soon as I can."

"Thank you, Miss Badger." He nodded and let himself out. The old screen door swung back and slammed on its wooden frame. I watched McKay back the large black and white Chevrolet out of the driveway and turn right, picking up speed as he turned onto the main road and headed back towards O'Halleran Bay's downtown area. I leaned in the doorway and gazed at the large expanse of grass, newly green from the recent spring rain, that led down a slight hill to a sandy beach and the waters of Cedar Lake. I thought briefly about digging up the azaleas to check for a body in the flower bed but the thought passed and, after a cup of coffee and another cigarette, I went back to bed.

Two years before my father died he bought a beautiful black Ford Super Deluxe sedan that had, along with the house on Albany Street in Toronto and the cottage in O'Halleran Bay, become part of my inheritance. It was hardly the car I wanted to drive at the age of twenty-eight (I envisioned myself bombing around town in a convertible, something in a bright blue) but it was a gorgeous car and, admittedly, much more appropriate for Canadian winters than a convertible. It was Thursday morning, almost a week after Corporal McKay's visit, when I pulled the Ford into a spot in front of the small building that housed the O'Halleran Bay Police Force. From the seat beside me, I grabbed an old leather satchel I'd stuffed full of my father's notebooks and slipped my handbag over my arm. The downtown streets were busy with housewives and businessmen moving swiftly from store to store and shopkeepers sweeping the sidewalks and putting out displays. I knew it would be less than a month before the Bay was flooded with campers and summer vacationers, either up for a day of fishing or boating or up for several weeks to stay at the local cabins, campgrounds or lodges. I pushed open the door to the police station and hit an older woman in the back.

"Excuse me," I apologized.

She gave me a disapproving look. "I'm in line. You're after me."

I smiled at the old crank pot. "Of course."

The small front office couldn't accommodate more than the five people already crowded inside. We stood waiting in front of a tall counter with a scarred wooden top that took up most of the wall opposite the doors. At the end of the counter was a closed wooden gate that separated the front office from the rest of the station. Behind the counter, two desks stood opposite each other, one on either side of the room. A mismatched collection of filing cabinets were placed along the walls, their tops piled high with paper. At the back of the large room were two closed doors. One door had "Chief A. Parsons" painted on the frosted glass, the other door was windowless. Beside those two rooms was another, smaller open area with a table and a set of hooks on the wall. A door propped open with a large metal sculpture of a dog carrying slippers revealed the beginnings of a corridor with red brick walls, presumably leading to the cells. That was it. That was the O'Halleran Bay police station in 1946.

There was no one behind the desk. I had just made up my mind to leave and come back another day when Chief A. Parsons' door rattled open and an incredibly tall, incredibly wide man clomped

15

noisily into the open area behind the desk. His brown hair and moustache were neatly combed and his suit was pressed but there was something about him that seemed rushed and haphazard, as if he might inadvertently trip over his own feet and fall. As long as I knew him (and I knew Bertie for decades) he always reminded me of a hardboiled egg sitting in a very small egg cup. He eyed the large group of people waiting in the front office.

"Where's Wagner? He's supposed to be at the desk," he barked. His large black shoes thudded on the floor as he made his way over to the radio transmitter that was set up behind one of the desks. Fingers the size of sausages turned the dials left and right and tapped the microphone. "Boucher and McKay return to the station. Boucher and McKay return to the station." He looked over at us. "Did that work? Did you hear anything?"

A man standing at the counter just shrugged his shoulders.

"What in blue blazes!" the Chief yelled. He twisted the dials to the left, then all the way to the right, all the while turning the microphone switch on and off. "Wagner!" he bellowed. He fiddled with the radio some more. "Boucher! McKay! Station! Now!" he yelled into the microphone.

We'd used two-way radios during the war but in 1946 the O'Halleran Bay Police Force only had a one-way radio. It operated using the same frequency as the local radio station so at any moment the police could interrupt your radio programme with a message asking a constable to go to a certain address, stop a specific car or return to the station. Since communication was only one way, there was no immediate way to tell if the police officer heard the message. At that point, we were at least five years away from getting two-way radios in little old O'Halleran Bay.

Somewhere in the background, an off-key version of "We'll Meet Again" started and got gradually louder until a man in a rumpled suit came through the doorway from the brick corridor, his hands secured behind him by a stout, middle-aged man in a sergeant's uniform, his slightly pockmarked face screwed into a scowl.

"What's going on? Why aren't you at the desk?" the Chief shouted.

"We've got two jail cells, fourteen prisoners and this guy decides to be smart and start up trouble," the sergeant answered.

"This radio!" On, off, on, off went the microphone switch. "Take him to the interview room. Leave the cuffs on him. What am I supposed to do with this?"

17

the Chief asked the crowded room, not pausing for a breath in between his instructions and his question.

I may have lied about being a stenographer but I was trained in radio operations before I was liberated from the CWACs and given other work to do. I stepped around the miserable crone in front of me and marched over to the gate that separated the front office from the rest of the police station. Reaching over and lifting the latch, I let myself into the station and marched brusquely over to the radio. I took the microphone from the Chief's hand, put one earpiece from the headset to my ear and adjusted the radio controls. Finally, I stuck the microphone near his mouth. "Talk," I told him, flicking the switch.

He stared. Then he bellowed. "Boucher, McKay return to the station. Boucher, McKay return to the station." He looked at me. "Did it go through?"

I turned off the microphone and put it down on the table. "It went through, alright."

"You stay on that side of the desk," the Chief motioned. "Wagner, get up to that desk and get rid of these people!"

Returning from a room at the back of the station, Wagner sighed loudly. "Yes, Chief."

The Chief grabbed his hat from his office and clomped to the back of the station. A door closed loudly. I let myself back out the gate and returned to my place in line behind the old crank pot. The man at the front of the line wanted to report his wallet stolen but after describing it and every single object that was in it (including a ticket stub for the previous Saturday's double feature), he decided that perhaps it wasn't stolen after all and would go home and ask his wife if it was in his blue pants. Next was a woman who had a pair of pants and a shirt stolen from her clothesline and wanted to know what kind of world we were living in when someone steals a pair of pants and a shirt right off a clothesline. I knew exactly what kind of world we were living in, had seen it for myself and could say with great certainty that a stolen pair of pants and a shirt from a clothesline in O'Halleran Bay, Ontario, Canada was quite minor when compared to what had just transpired, what was still transpiring, in the rest of the world. The next man wanted to report that his car had been hit by a red truck when it was parked on a side street. This, of course, led to a long discussion and intense speculation about all those in town who drove a red truck and would have the lack of character to keep driving after damaging someone else's property. The line seemed to move ahead in microscopic increments. Fifteen minutes passed, then twenty.

Sergeant Wagner looked up when the woman in front of me stepped up to the counter and set her large handbag on top of his paperwork.

"Mrs. Webster," he said. "What can I help you with today?"

"Carl, I'm here today just like I have been every Thursday since December when those Peterson boys got that car of theirs."

"Mrs. Webster, we can't arrest the Peterson boys for something they might do," Wagner told her firmly.

She ignored him and went on. "Every Friday and Saturday evening they drive their car up and down the road as if they're in a race, cutting the corner and running over part of my lawn."

"The Petersons are cutting the corner and running over part of the boulevard which is owned by the town. However, as we tell you every Thursday, we cannot spare a constable to sit at the corner every Friday and Saturday night until one of the Peterson boys speeds or drives over the boulevard just so we can give him a ticket."

"I suppose law-abiding citizens don't have any rights anymore?"

"Constables have talked to your neighbours, Mrs. Webster, and none of them have seen the boys doing more than twenty-five miles per hour down your street."

"Which is five miles per hour over the speed limit," she retorted. Angrily, she grabbed her handbag and settled it in the crook of her arm. She sniffed. "Since you refuse to take my request seriously, I will once again have to talk this over with Chief Parsons after church on Sunday." She turned on her heel and stomped out of the vestibule, her comfortable black shoes squeaking slightly as she passed me.

I turned around and waited until the wooden door swung shut behind her. "I'm sure living next to her is a gas."

Wagner rolled his eyes. "If I were one of the Peterson boys, I'd drive over her front lawn, back up and drive over it again."

"I'm just here to drop off some papers Corporal McKay requested," I set the satchel on the desk and turned to leave.

The door to the station opened and McKay stalked in.

"You were supposed to relieve me an hour ago," McKay told Wagner.

"I've been stuck here. Why didn't you call in?" Wagner asked.

"I tried three times but the line was busy. By the way, the Chief should probably know that the call box down at the lake isn't working. I had to go into Cedar Lake Lodge and use the phone there."

"Didn't you hear? The Mayor has done away with all of the call boxes in town. We're a modern police force now. We have the radio." Wagner gestured grandly to the radio transmitter behind him.

"Done away with the call boxes? How are we supposed to contact the station? Never mind that, how are we supposed to hear the call over the radio when we've only got one police car and the Chief is usually driving it?" Finally seeing me, McKay took off his cap. "Miss Badger."

"Corporal," I handed him the satchel. "My father's notebooks from 1941. I don't know if they'll be any help but you're welcome to look. If you don't mind, I'd like them back when you're done."

"Of course," he nodded. "And thanks for the C int C angle. The Chief's looking into it." He looked at Wagner. "This is Miss Arvilla Badger, Doctor Badger's daughter. Miss Badger was a CWAC. She served overseas."

"That would explain how you knew how to work the radio," Wagner said.

"The Chief was having trouble," I explained to McKay.

McKay winced. "We try to keep him away from the radio."

The door to the station opened again and a stocky blond man wearing a blue O'Halleran Bay Police Force uniform hurried in. Ignoring Wagner and McKay, he smiled at me and held my gaze. I sized him up right away. He was the sort who knew he was attractive and took every opportunity to try and work his charm on anything wearing a skirt.

"Where were you?" Wagner asked.

"I was all the way over on Bridge Road when the call went out. Mrs. Bowles heard it on the radio and yelled out as I was walking past her place," he answered.

"You better get over to Wainwright Metals right away. Some union guys from Toronto showed up and are making trouble. Wainwright himself just called. He's fit to be tied. The Chief and Stewart are over there," Wagner told him.

"If Stewart's over there, why does he need me?" he sighed.

"For entertainment," Wagner told him. "Get moving, Boucher."

Boucher winked at me then sauntered back out the front doors of the station.

"Busy place around here," I remarked, turning to leave.

"Wait until the summer." He looked at Wagner. "What do you need me for?"

He held up a stack of papers. "I've got fourteen Catholics in the cells that I need to write up and release before it's time for church or I'll have to listen to Father Donovan. Then I have to get the duty roster done this afternoon."

McKay shook his head. "Not this afternoon. I'm supposed to be working on the Adams case this afternoon. The notes from the Toronto Police and a copy of the report Mr. and Mrs. Adams filed just came this morning."

"Take it home. Read it tonight. It'll be a nice bed-time story," Wagner shrugged.

"Where's the new kid the Chief just hired? Brown or whatever his name is?" McKay said.

"His name was Henry Black and he quit," Wagner told him.

"He was only here a day," McKay said.

"Apparently that was one day too many," Wagner answered.

I shifted my handbag to my other arm. "You're very busy. I'll leave you to your work. Good day, Corporal. Sergeant."

McKay reached out and placed a hand on my elbow. "Say, you think you could stick around?"

I shrugged my arm, sending his hand back to his side. "What for?"

He looked at Wagner. "What about Miss Badger working at the desk?"

Wagner whistled. "The Chief will never go for it."

"During the war there were three women working in the office, taking reports and answering the phone. What's the big deal anyway?"

"That was during the war. There was a shortage of manpower. And one of those women was the Chief's wife."

"Open your eyes, Wagner. There's still a shortage of manpower. We're short of constables as it is and you know the population almost doubles in size during the summer. Why should a constable spend all summer answering the phone and taking reports about lost wallets and noise complaints? Not to mention the filing. We're up to our eyeballs in filing. I recite the alphabet in my sleep. We'll be working fifty to sixty-hour weeks as it is."

"We can get MacInnis to come in a few more days a week," Wagner suggested.

"Are you kidding? He's working as a lifeguard over at Cedar Lake Lodge making ten dollars a day," McKay said.

"Ten dollars? A day? To look at a bunch of ladies in swimsuits?" Wagner asked, incredulous.

"I think he's supposed to make sure no one drowns, not just ogle the girls in swimsuits," I said.

"My mother wanted me to take swimming lessons. I wanted to join the Boy Scouts. I should have listened to my mother," he shook his head.

McKay opened the gate that separated the front from the back offices. "What do you think? Are you interested?"

I hesitated then walked through the gate and sat down in a chair beside one of the desks. "I think you should check with your Chief first."

Wagner let out a long rush of breath. "The Chief isn't going to like this."

McKay said down on the edge of the desk. "The Chief hasn't liked anything since the Great War."

Wagner smiled at the prospect but quickly shook his head. "He'll never go for it."

The sound of the back door opening and slamming shut made the three of us peer towards the back of the station. The Chief, Boucher and another man, thin and sour-looking, clomped into the office.

"Everything alright at Wainwright, sir?" Wagner asked.

"It's handled for now. I sent the labour organizers back to Toronto, bunch of Reds. As always, Boucher was a great help. By the time he showed up, it was over."

"I was all the way over on Bridge Road," Boucher complained.

"I don't even know why we have that radio. It hasn't made anyone move any faster." Eyeing me he said, "You're on the wrong side of the desk again, Miss."

"This is Miss Arvilla Badger, Chief," McKay said.

"Corporal, kindly escort Miss Badger to the other side of the desk," the Chief nodded and began to walk away.

"Miss Badger was a CWAC. She was trained in radio transmissions and spent much of the war working as a stenographer at military headquarters," McKay said.

"Lovely. Thank you for your service," Chief Parsons said, taking off his hat and tossing it into his open office. He opened the door to the room where Wagner had stored the drunk and looked in. "Boucher, get this man down to the cells. He's drooling on the table."

"Miss Badger has an exemplary service record and is thoroughly trained on the radio. I thought she might be just what we need, Chief. What about Miss Badger working at the desk?" McKay asked.

"What desk?"

"This desk. The desk here. To free up Wagner."

"No." Without looking at anyone, Parsons continued making his way to the other side of the smaller room with the table and hooks where I could see now that a kitchenette with a small stove and some cupboards were set up.

"Come on, Bertie. We're drowning here," McKay pleaded. "She could handle the paperwork and answer the phone."

"That will be the job of the recruit I'm hiring."

"What recruit?" McKay asked.

"We've had some interest. A few men have applied," Parsons said.

"Larry Anderson," Wagner chimed in.

"Larry Anderson? Fat Larry Anderson with asthma? Yeah. He'll be a real asset to the force," McKay said.

"There was that other kid too. What was his name? Munroe?" Boucher spoke up, dropping into a chair and casually resting his feet on the desk across from me.

"His mother brought him in here and asked the Chief to give him a job, for God's sake. Oh, yeah, we've had some real prospects," McKay said.

"We'll never get anyone with the kind of money this city pays. Do you know the night watchman over at Wainwright Metals gets a dollar an hour?" Boucher said.

"I heard a dollar and a quarter," Wagner said.

"Plus he gets two free dinners a week at the cantine," Boucher added.

"A dollar and a quarter? What am I doing working here?" McKay said.

"And in the summer he's allowed to wear short sleeves instead of a wool tunic."

"You just want to wear short sleeves so the girls can see your muscles," McKay told him.

"The city won't authorize more money. We've been over this." Parsons filled the kettle with water and set it back on the hob. He turned the burner on and it flared bright orange.

The thin constable opened a drawer of the tall metal filing cabinet to the left of the desk and took a paper from a large stack that sat on top. He crisply shoved the paper into a folder. "I don't approve of women working. They should stay in the house where they belong."

"Stewart lives with his mother," Wagner told me.

"When he goes to work he chains her to the front of the house," Boucher laughed.

"Don't worry. He leaves her plenty of water," McKay added.

The Chief sighed and scrubbed his face with his hands. "Get back to work. Let me have my tea in peace."

I stood up. "Thank you, Corporal McKay. I hope you find my father's notebooks useful. Good day, gentlemen."

"We certainly don't need Miss Badger. The Chief is perfectly capable of working the desk and phone all by himself Saturdays." Wagner said casually.

"Saturday? What Saturday?" Parsons asked, suddenly alert.

"I'm away the first Friday, Saturday and Sunday of June, July and August for militia training. Remember? I submitted my papers in April," Wagner said.

"Yes. Yes. Militia training. Of course," Parsons muttered. "Those damn Russians. I suppose we have to be ready in case they make their move. But why am I working the desk?"

"I had to shuffle the duty roster to cover my shifts, Chief. Everyone else is already working over their maximum allotted hours. You were the only one left."

"What about MacInnis?" Parsons asked.

"He's already working weekends at Cedar Lake Lodge and he won't give it up. It pays more." Boucher said.

"You could walk the beat and the other man on duty could work the desk," Wagner offered.

"I suppose I can manage for three weekends this summer," Parsons said quickly.

"It's actually a total of six weekends, Chief. I have militia training too, the last weekend of every month," Boucher said.

"Six weekends." McKay whistled. "That's half of the summer standing behind the desk."

"Seven weekends," Stewart corrected him, waving a piece of paper in the air. "I have a signed authorization for time off on August 15 and 16."

"Visiting family that weekend, Stewart? The circus must be in town," Boucher said.

"For your information, I'm escorting Mother to my cousin's wedding in Kingston," Stewart replied.

"The Chief has the right idea. He's putting himself right in the thick of things. The public will love the fact that they'll be able to come in and go directly to the Chief of Police with their complaints and problems. The Chief will be able to deal with everything straight away. Not to mention the fact that he'll be able to keep up to date on paperwork. The next shift will relieve him at six. That's plenty of time to get a little fishing done before the sun sets. It's a good move, Chief, if you ask me," Wagner said.

Oh, Wagner. He may have looked like a dog's ass end but he was damn clever.

I was almost out the door when I heard the loud clatter of Parsons' tea cup and saucer on the table.

"Miss Badger!" I turned and Parsons threw up his hands in exasperation. "I'm not promising you anything."

I stared at him without flinching.

"I'll have to square it with the town council and they've already warned me they're not inclined to spend any more money on policing this year. I might be able to convince them to fund a temporary position, maybe for a few months at the most but I wouldn't get my hopes up. Keep in mind that the job would consist of paperwork and answering the telephone; extremely dull work," he warned me.

I crossed my arms and looked him over. "Well, you're in luck, Chief Parsons. After four years overseas I'm very much looking forward to dull work."

Two

That was how I started working for the O'Halleran Bay Police Force in the spring of 1946 for three mornings a week and Saturdays at forty-seven cents an hour. I heard many years later that the city council wanted to pay me forty cents an hour but Albert Parsons managed to get them to agree to forty-seven. I always liked Bertie for that. It was still twenty cents less per hour than the men were making in the factory but that's the way it was those days.

I accepted the job not because I really wanted it or even because I needed it. My father's death (and my mother's years before) had left me enough money to live on, for a while at least. The honest truth of it was that I was at loose ends after the war. I had returned to Toronto in the summer of 1945 and spent the first three months growing accustomed to civilian life again. A fair amount of that time was spent drinking and carrying on, celebrating the war's end with old friends who had also returned and were trying to fit back into the lives they'd had before the war. It took me about a week to realize that the life I'd had before no longer existed. I mean, really, how could it? I was twenty-two when I joined up, fresh out of university. My entire life consisted of studying, going to student dances, attending house parties and picnics and spending Saturdays lounging in the women's common room. I had returned from Britain at twenty-eight years old, without direction or a purpose. I didn't quite know what to do with myself and I don't think the world quite knew what to do with me.

The work for the Bay Police was uncomplicated but tedious. Wagner relinquished control of his desk for exactly one hour every morning to do whatever it was he needed to do, though he did so cautiously at first, typing slowly with two fingers and pretending not to listen while I handled basic public inquiries (Where do I get a license for my dog?) and complaints (Someone is dumping trash in the bushes on North Street), fearing that perhaps I wouldn't be able to deal with such taxing issues.

When he finished his work, he left me alone to answer the phone and to file the stacks of paperwork that I'm sure had been piling up since before the war.

I hadn't even been there a week when Parsons stuck his head out of his office one morning and bellowed, "McKay, Lawrence Adams and his family are at their summer house this week. I've asked them to come in on Friday so you can take a full statement. Where's Miss Badger?" Without missing a beat, he turned to me. "Miss Badger, you'll sit in on the interview and take meticulous notes. I don't want any detail missed. Type it all up in a report when you're done and give it to McKay. There will likely be a lot of crying from Mrs. Adams and her daughter. Bring a handkerchief or two." His door slammed shut.

That Friday morning when Charlotte Adams walked through the front door of the O'Halleran Bay Police station, I knew just by looking at her that I wouldn't need the handkerchief. Tall and lithe, she glided into the station and past the desks, into the interrogation room with an air that was part annoyance and part superiority. Women like that didn't cry in public. Lawrence Adams followed behind her, stoically smoking a cigarette and walking with his daughter, a young woman who looked to be about twenty.

Mrs. Adams paused just long enough beside the large table to make it clear she expected McKay to pull out her chair. After he obliged, she sat down and removed her gloves, sitting them beside her purse in one crisp movement. Her daughter sat down beside her and Mr. Adams leaned up against the wall near the door. I moved past him and sat down in a chair in the opposite corner where I could observe everyone. (And pretend to take notes because I hadn't the faintest idea how to write in shorthand.)

"Have you found my son?" Mrs. Adams demanded.

McKay sat down in a chair across from her and placed his notebook on the table. "No, Mrs. Adams. Not yet."

"Then what are we doing here?" she snapped.

"Charlotte. For God's sake," Mr. Adams sighed.

"I would like you to tell me everything you can remember about the days leading up to and following Hugh's disappearance," McKay said.

"We've already told the police in Toronto everything we know. Last week," Mrs. Adams said impatiently. "Why can't you just read their report?"

"I did," McKay assured her. "But if I'm to start an investigation I want to rely upon first-hand information, not information that may have been misinterpreted by another constable."

"If you start an investigation?" Mrs. Adams repeated. "For the love of God! I suppose you think my son just walked away that night and started a new life somewhere else? My son is missing," she enunciated the word slowly, "and this is not helping to find him."

The daughter reached over and took her mother's hand. "Mother, please. The constable is just trying to help."

"Actually, I'm a Corporal," McKay said. "Let's go back to July 1941. Was the whole family here in O'Halleran Bay?"

Mr. Adams nodded. "Charlotte and the children came up at the end of June, just as they always had. They stay for the entire summer, right up until the week before the children start back at school. That summer I came up for Dominion Day and was supposed to stay until the end of July."

"But Hugh wasn't a child that summer. He had just finished law school." McKay prompted.

"Yes. He was supposed to start with my firm in Toronto at the end of August," his father said.

"Was he happy about that?" McKay asked.

"Of course he was," Mrs. Adams said.

"Was Hugh happy about starting his law career, Mr. Adams? Did he seem happy or excited about working with you in the fall?" McKay asked pointedly.

"I don't know," Lawrence Adams finally admitted after a pause. "My son and I hadn't seen eye to eye in some time. He didn't reveal much to me."

"And Miss Adams, what about you?" McKay asked.

She nodded. "I was only fifteen at the time. Hugh was almost twenty-four. He doted on me because I was his little sister but he didn't tell me much."

"It says in the Toronto police report that Hugh invited some friends to spend two weeks in O'Halleran Bay; Barbara Fisher, Ellen Hale and William Llewellyn and that you rented a cottage from Mr. Badger for them. Why did you rent a cottage, Mr. Adams? You have a large summer home here that could have accommodated everyone," McKay said.

"That isn't entirely true," Mrs. Adams answered. "Hugh had been going with Barbara Fisher for about three years. I thought their relationship was serious and since they had both graduated that spring I assumed they would want to get married soon. Mr. Adams and I had never even met the young lady so I suggested Hugh invite her to stay with us for a few weeks in July. She was supposed to stay at our house in Dorothy's room but at the last minute Hugh told us that Bill and one of Barbara's friends were coming too. Hugh insisted that the girls were going to stay at Cedar Lake Lodge but it was full that week so it was Hugh who ended up renting the cottage. I didn't feel it was appropriate but Hugh informed me that I should just mind my own business."

I hastily scribbled down everything I could on a notepad.

"The report to the Toronto police doesn't include any information about Hugh's friends who were visiting. Let's start with Barbara Fisher. What do you know about her? Do you know how I could get in contact with her?" McKay asked.

"Truthfully, we don't know anything about her except that Hugh met her at university. She was studying the humanities or something." Mr. Adams said.

"And her friend?"

"Ellen Hale was getting her teaching certificate," Mrs. Adams said. "I got the feeling that Hugh didn't like her and that the feeling was mutual. I think she mentioned that she and Barbara were childhood friends and that they were from Toronto. I know there was no love lost between her and Bill, that was plain. They never stopped sniping at each other."

"When did everyone arrive in O'Halleran Bay?"

"Hugh went to Toronto and picked the girls up in his car. They arrived on Saturday. Bill arrived a few days later. Monday I believe."

McKay flipped through an old calendar. "Would that have been July fifth, twelfth or nineteenth?"

"It was the twelfth. The girls were supposed to stay for two weeks and then return to Toronto with me on the twenty-eighth," Mr. Adams said.

"Alright. During those two weeks does anything stick out in your mind? Anything different or out of the ordinary? What did Hugh and his friends do during that time?"

"Everything was perfectly normal," Mrs. Adams said. "Though, after a few days, Hugh and I did have words. I'd hardly seen Barbara for more than an hour. They were always running off to the beach or playing tennis or going dancing. Hugh would stay out until all hours and then sleep late."

"Charlotte, a young man does not want to be tied to his mother's apron strings. He wants to be out carousing with his pretty girl," Mr. Adams said.

"They were always at the cottage. I didn't feel it was appropriate and I said so to Hugh. If she were my daughter, Barbara certainly wouldn't be staying out until all hours at a cottage unchaperoned. But she wasn't my daughter so what could I do?"

"When did you notice that Hugh was missing?" McKay asked.

"The last Saturday of their visit, they went sailing and took Dorothy along. They came back to the house for supper and left soon after which I thought was rude," Mrs. Adams said.

"There was a dance at the Lodge that night and they had to get ready," Mr. Adams explained. "Sunday evening the girls called asking whether Hugh was at our house. They said they hadn't seen him since about midnight Sunday morning when he and Barbara fought and he stormed off. The girls had been trying to reach him all day but no one answered the phone. We were visiting friends Sunday and had only just arrived home. I started driving around the Bay looking for him and found his car in the lot at the train station."

"I have since learned that it was a common occurrence for Barbara and Hugh to fight, especially when they were drinking," Mrs. Adams added.

"Did they drink a lot?" McKay asked.

Mr. Adams shrugged.

"You'd have to ask Barbara or their friends. I really wouldn't know," Mrs. Adams answered.

"Did you see Hugh Sunday morning before you left?" McKay asked.

"He wasn't home. His car wasn't in the driveway and he wasn't in his bedroom," Mr. Adams said.

"We assumed he'd spent the night with Barbara." Mrs. Adams' disapproving look towards her daughter served as a warning, leaving no doubt as to her thoughts about young ladies who entertained men overnight.

McKay jotted a few notes down on his paper. "Where was Bill during this time?"

"He'd already gone. He only stayed in O'Halleran Bay for about a week; nine days at the most. He had to report for basic training," Mr. Adams said.

"What was the make and model of Hugh's car?" McKay asked.

"It was a 1936 Chevrolet, cream-coloured two-door coupe. It had a green panel over the rear passenger side tire and a dent in the front driver's door," Adams said. "I sold it about three years ago but I may still have the name of the kid I sold it to if you need it."

McKay shook his head. "It's unlikely the car itself would be of any use at this point but I plan to ask around town to see if anyone remembers seeing it on Sunday morning but honestly it's been five years so I'm not optimistic I'll get many responses. Did you contact the police when you couldn't find your son, Mr. Adams?"

Lawrence Adams rose from the wall where he'd been leaning and reached over his wife to stub out his cigarette in the ashtray on the table. "No. Since his clothing and wallet were missing we assumed he'd run off to enlist."

"When war broke out he wanted to enlist. He was in the middle of his education and I begged him to wait," Mrs. Adams explained.

"I insisted he finish his education first," Mr. Adams added. "I wanted him to secure his future. Ever since he'd entered his last year at university, he'd been making noise about enlisting. We fought constantly about it but we had a particularly bad row about it just before he came up to the Bay. He told me that he was tired of me controlling his life and that he didn't need my permission to enlist. He threatened that one day he'd just be gone."

"And you thought he'd made good on that threat," McKay concluded, sitting back in his chair and dropping the pencil beside his leather notebook.

"Later, we received two postcards from him," Mrs. Adams said, reaching into her handbag and pulling out two stiff pieces of cardboard. She handed them to McKay and he turned them over, examining each side carefully.

"Is this Hugh's handwriting?" he asked.

"I think so," Mrs. Adams said.

Mr. Adams nodded.

"We waited for Hugh to come home after the War but when he didn't contact us, I became concerned. I just wanted to know that he was alive and well. I wanted him to know that even if he chose not to speak to Mother and Father there was no reason to shut me out too. I went to a Department of Defense office fearing the worst. I thought perhaps he'd been killed in action and we hadn't been notified. They told me that he'd never enlisted. Father made inquiries too and was told the same thing," Dorothy said.

"Have any of his friends heard from him?" McKay asked.

"We don't know many of Hugh's friends but the ones we were able to contact haven't heard from him," his father replied.

"One last thing for today. Do you think that I'd be able to search his room?"

Mr. Adams shook his head. "He hadn't used his room at the summer house in years."

"What about your house in Toronto?"

"We left his room exactly as it was. I wanted it to be just the way he remembered it when he came home from Europe." Mrs. Adams made it sound like her son was off touring the great sites of Europe instead of fighting a war.

McKay stood and shook Mr. Adams' hand. "Thank you for coming in. I want you to know I'll do everything I can to locate your son."

Lawrence Adams nodded automatically and thanked McKay but the expression on his thin face seemed less than hopeful. Mrs. Adams slipped her arm through her daughter's and walked ahead of her husband, through the station and out the door.

I stood up and joined McKay at the table, picking up one of the postcards and examining it. It was a painted illustration of a pink mailbox, a cream coloured envelope sticking out of it. Lavender, light blue and white flowers entwined with lush greenery decorated the rest of the card.

"You ever send a card this sappy?" I asked.

McKay grinned and shrugged. "He was sending it to his mother."

"This one's even worse." I pointed to the other postcard and scoffed. It was a Christmas scene with a little white kitten in front of a pink Christmas tree, a large pink bow tied around its neck and a light blue Christmas ball in its mouth. "These aren't the type of postcards you send to your mother. These are the type of postcards you send to your girl." I picked up the postcards and turned them over, examining them carefully, seeing for the first time the inconsistencies neither of us had seen before.

He shrugged again. "Maybe."

"How many postcards did you send during the War?" I asked him.

"A few."

I held up the Christmas postcard and pointed to the stamp on the front, partially obscuring the top of the Christmas tree. "Did you ever put a stamp on the front of the postcard, on the side with the picture?"

"No," he admitted.

"The stamp on a postcard goes on the back, on the blank side in the corner above the name and address," I said. "These aren't even postcards. Look," I pointed to the bottom edge of both pieces of paper. "Someone has cut these. You can see a very faint pencil line that was drawn on the paper and used as a cutting guide. I think they might have been greeting cards."

McKay took the postcard in his hand and peered at it closely. "You're a regular Nancy Drew."

It was my turn to grin. "Thanks but I'd rather be Nora Charles. She has better dialogue and much more fun."

He handed the postcard back to me. "It's not that odd. Sometimes you had to use whatever you could get your hands on to write a letter or send a note."

I held up the postcard with the mailbox and flowers. "This one's postmarked Brockville. All officers were trained in Brockville from 1940 onwards. It should be easy enough to find out if Hugh Adams was there." I looked at the other postcard. "This was mailed from England."

"I'll check into Brockville, of course, but Lawrence and Dorothy Adams were both told that Hugh never enlisted," he said. "What about you? You went to the University of Toronto at the same time as Adams and his friends. Any of these names ring a bell? Mrs. Adams said Barbara was studying the Humanities. Maybe you had a class with her?"

I shook my head. "Her name isn't familiar but the next time I go to Toronto, I'll bring back my yearbooks. Maybe if I see her picture I'll recognize her from a class or remember seeing her around campus. She didn't live at Whitney Hall with me, that's for sure."

McKay looked down at my open notebook and pointed to the page of scribbles and doodles, single words written haphazardly all over the page. "I've never seen that kind of shorthand before. Did they teach you that in the army?"

Hastily, I took up the notepad and stuck it under my arm. "I'll have the notes from the interview typed up for you directly," I told him.

And that was probably the day I found out two very important things about Joe McKay. The first was that for all his aw-shucks-ma'am small-town deputy routine, he was quite sharp. The second, which would prove to impact our friendship the most, was that McKay always kept his cards close to his chest.

Three

I 've always thought that the simplest explanation is usually the correct one which led me to believe that Adams had probably run off and enlisted. Maybe he used an alternate spelling of his first or last name. Maybe he had a note attached to his file requesting that information not be released, even upon his death. More than likely, though, this was a case of misplaced paperwork. This was 1946, remember. There wasn't a database. You couldn't just turn on a computer and type in names. Every enlisted person had a manilla file folder in a cabinet somewhere in a warehouse in Ottawa. It wasn't hard for me to believe that some dum dum had looked in the wrong place. I thought it was probably a good idea for McKay to send another request for information. I had seen enough of the army to know that if you ask a question three times you'd likely get three different answers.

At this point, the only thing I found odd about the whole case was the postcards. I turned the details of those two cards over and over in my mind even after I dropped into bed that night. Why was the postage on the front of the postcard? The illustrations on the postcards suggested they may have been meant for Barbara Fisher but if that was the case, why were they sent to Mr. and Mrs. Adams? It seemed to me that the next step in McKay's investigation was to talk to Adams' friends, people he might have contacted after he left, people he would tell things he wouldn't or couldn't tell his parents and by the time I woke up the next morning, I'd already figured out a way to locate Barbara Fisher, Ellen Hale and Bill Llewellyn.

It really was my intention to tell McKay my plan and let him handle it but when I got to the station that morning he had already gone on patrol. I waited for twenty minutes after I was done work at noon but he still hadn't returned. Wagner knew I was up to something when I sat down at McKay's desk, picked up the phone and called the operator but he just shook his head and ignored me.

McKay walked into the station late that afternoon, wiping the sweat from his forehead. "Only May and it's already this hot. I can't wait until July." He took off his tunic and stood in front of the fan that Wagner had spent fifteen minutes positioning perfectly to avoid disturbing any of the papers on his desk while still circulating cool air around him.

Wagner made a face. "God, man. Change your shirt. You stink."

"I'm off in ten minutes," McKay said.

"You may want to change your mind and your shirt after you hear this," I said.

McKay looked up and saw me sitting at the table with a cup of coffee and a notebook. "Miss Badger, what are you still doing here? Weren't you off at noon?" he asked, draping his tunic on the back of his chair.

I picked up my notebook, crossed the room and sat down on the corner of McKay's desk. "I've been on the horn and at the library all afternoon. I found contact information for Ellen Hale, Barbara Fisher and Bill Llewellyn."

"Miss Badger, it wasn't your place to do that," he warned me angrily.

I crossed my arms across my chest. "You want the information or not?"

51

He sighed. "Alright. I'll bite. What did you find out?"

"I called the University of Toronto and managed to weasel some information out of a very nasty woman working in the alumni office. They had phone numbers and addresses for Bill and Barbara. The number they had for Bill was his parents' home. I talked to his mother. He doesn't live there currently but she promised that she'd let him know the O'Halleran Bay Police want to talk to him the next time she sees him. She was pretty tight-lipped when I asked for an address and I got the feeling Bill doesn't have a fixed address. The number for Barbara was out of service so I searched the phone directory until I found someone who lives in the same building as the Fishers. I talked to a woman in apartment fourteen. She said that they moved out about three years ago and she doesn't know where they went. All of this is pretty disappointing so far but I struck oil with Ellen Hale. She contacted the university about a year ago to change her name and address. She lives at 54 Champlain Street, right here in O'Halleran Bay."

"Here?"

"Yes. Which is the reason I had to go to the library. I found her wedding announcement in the Bay Gazette. It took up two-thirds of an entire page and included a large photo of the happy couple. There was paragraph after paragraph about Cupid and true love with a few Bible verses thrown in. It was love at first sight when Henry saw Ellen at a dance at Cedar Lake Lodge in the summer of 1941. She waited patiently for him to return from Europe, fearing every day for his safety until he finally returned, a hero in the fight against Fascism. It was the most sentimental drivel I've seen since the last Bette Davis movie. The details of the actual Cardiff - Hale wedding took up several more paragraphs.

"Wait a minute. She married Henry Cardiff?"

"Yes. You know him?"

"We went to high school together. He goes by Hank. He sells insurance now. His office is just off of Main Street."

"I'm heading home," I said, gathering my gloves, hat and handbag from the large table at the back of the station. "Hurry up and change your shirt and I'll give you a ride over to Champlain Street."

"I've got my motorcycle," McKay said.

"Is that what you call that hunk of rusted metal?"

He smiled but said nothing. Taking a clean white shirt from one of the hooks at the back, McKay went into the washroom to change.

Just why he took me up on the offer of a ride to Champlain Street, I never did find out. My reason for offering to drive him was as transparent as Tallulah Bankhead's drawers: I wanted to be there when he questioned Ellen Hale. It seemed only right since I'd done all the work to find the damn woman in the first place and I was curious to see if she could offer any other clues to Hugh Adams' whereabouts. But it was more than all this, I realize now. I felt *interested*, thoroughly and completely engrossed in the details of this case and it had been months since I'd felt awake enough to have a genuine interest in anything.

Champlain Street was at the north end of town, in a newly developed area of modest homes on large lots. Number fifty-four was a two-level red brick house with two dormers at the front. There was no car in the driveway but the windows and screen door were open.

"Thanks for the ride," McKay said. "You don't need to wait. I'll hoof it back to the station when I'm done."

I put the car in park and turned off the engine. "I don't mind. In fact, I could help you by taking notes and typing up a summary of the interview. It'll save you the trouble."

McKay arched an eyebrow at me. "I knew there had to be a reason you offered me the ride. No. Forget it."

I grabbed my handbag in one hand and opened the car door with the other. "I don't mind."

McKay jumped out of the car and followed me as I made my way up the walkway to the front door. "I mind. And so will the Chief. Besides, your shorthand is terrible and you type slower than Wagner."

I knocked loudly on the door and quickly moved off to the side so McKay was front and centre when a young, well-dressed woman wearing an apron appeared.

"Yes?" she said.

"Ellen Cardiff?" McKay asked.

"I'm Mrs. Henry Cardiff."

"Corporal Joe McKay of the O'Halleran Bay police force." He gestured to me. "This is my...stenographer, Miss Arvilla Badger. May we come in?"

She looked us up and down. "What is this regarding? I haven't done anything wrong, I hope." There was something about her voice that seemed artificial, like she was talking to us in the tone she only brought out for company.

"Not at all Mrs. Cardiff," McKay assured her. "I'm hoping that you might have some information that could help in a case I'm working on."

"My goodness," she said, opening up the screen door. "I can't imagine I would know anything about a police matter."

McKay stepped inside the house and I followed, taking a small notepad and pencil out of my handbag to keep up the pretense that I was going to take notes.

"Please, come into the sitting room," Ellen said, taking off her apron. "May I offer you some tea?"

"No, thank you," McKay told her. "I don't think we'll be very long."

Ellen folded up her apron into a compact little square and placed it on the table next to the telephone. She turned to her left and led us into the living room. Ellen sat down in a pale blue wingback chair, crossed her ankles and arranged her dress around her. I sat down on one end of the chesterfield while McKay took the other. She looked at us expectantly.

"I'd like to ask you some questions about Hugh Adams," McKay started.

"Hugh Adams? Whatever for?" Ellen asked.

"The O'Halleran Bay police force is looking into Hugh's disappearance and you were one of the last people to see him."

"His disappearance?" she said, confused. "He ran off and enlisted, last I heard."

"There's no record that he ever enlisted and it appears that no one has seen him since you and Miss Fisher last saw him on July 26, 1941. The police force has been asked to investigate. You and Miss Fisher came up to O'Halleran Bay as guests of Mr. and Mrs. Adams, is that right?"

Ellen shook her head then reached up and carefully patted her dark hair back into place. "I wouldn't say that. Hugh invited Barbara to come up for a vacation but her father didn't think it was appropriate for her to go alone. He was right, of course, so Barbara asked me to accompany her. I guess that's when Hugh decided to include Bill. I didn't care for Hugh or Bill but Barbara was my oldest and dearest friend and I would have done anything for her so, naturally, I agreed to go. I assumed we would be staying with the Adams' in their summer home. I never would have agreed to go if I'd known we were staying at a cottage without a chaperone."

"You didn't like Hugh Adams? Why?" I asked, suddenly curious.

"He was completely wrong for Barbara but she couldn't see it," Ellen said. "I told her time and time again that Hugh had no intention of marrying her and if she didn't smarten up she was going to find herself in the worst kind of trouble an unmarried woman can get into. I don't mean to speak crassly but she was starting to get a bad reputation and, as you know, no man wants another's second-hand goods."

I clamped my mouth shut to keep from firing a retort using language no decent woman should know and instead wrote down the word "insufferable" on my notepad.

"Hugh's mother seemed to think that Hugh and Barbara were headed for marriage," McKay said.

Ellen laughed. "Absolutely not. I assure you that marriage wasn't what Hugh was after. Not that Barbara seemed to mind. They would carry on, going to parties, drinking, and staying out until all hours. Barbara told me Hugh would take her to dance halls and jazz clubs in less than desirable parts of the city where they would mix with all types of people. Even," she paused and then whispered, "Negroes." She shook her head. "Then after a few weeks of that nonsense they'd have a big, loud fight and Barbara would start going on dates with other young men for a few weeks or a month. Eventually, Hugh would call on her and the whole thing would start over again.

"Do you remember what happened the Saturday and Sunday Hugh went missing?" McKay asked.

"Of course I do," Ellen answered. "I remember every detail of that vacation. That's when I met my Henry. That Saturday, Hugh rented a sailboat and we spent the afternoon out on the water. We took Hugh's little sister with us. Bill had already gone back to Toronto by then. I was surprised that I had a good time; Hugh was sufferable. Barbara and I went back to the cottage and changed for dinner at his parents' house. After dinner, we went to Cedar Lake Lodge. I had met Hank there the previous Saturday and we'd seen each other a few times that week. We met up that night and I spent the whole night dancing with him. I could tell he was every inch the gentleman." She turned to me and smiled smugly. "My Hank served and was wounded in Italy."

"I didn't know. I'm sorry to hear that," McKay said.

"He recovered, thank the Lord," Ellen told him. "I'm sure you served as well?"

"Provost Corps." McKay nodded towards me. "Miss Badger served too."

She gave me a pitying smile. "Oh, you were one of those CWACs? That's very honourable. I was content to do my duty on the home front."

I smiled back. I erased "insufferable" from my notepad with excessive force and scattered eraser dust on Ellen's perfect blue chesterfield. I wrote "condescending cow".

Perhaps fearing what I might say, McKay asked "What happened next? After the dance?"

"Hugh wanted to drink so he and Barbara went to some tavern in the township. I allowed Henry to drive me back to the cottage."

"When did Barbara return?"

"It was almost two o'clock in the morning. They were in the sitting room fighting, of course, and woke me up. Hugh was falling down drunk and angry, shouting and acting irrationally. Barbara had been drinking too, I could tell, though she wasn't as far gone as Hugh. I went into the living room and turned on the lights and Barbara went to her room, shut the door and went to sleep. I pushed Hugh out on the porch and told him to go home or sleep in his car. I shut off the lights and locked the door."

"Do you know why he was angry?"

"I haven't a clue. He was raving. I think he might have been saying something about lying or liars. I don't know and honestly, it was two o'clock in the morning and I wasn't paying attention. He was slurring his words and didn't make much sense, which was nothing new."

"That was the last time you ever saw him?"

Ellen nodded. "When I woke up later that morning his car was gone. I assumed he'd driven home. I never saw him again."

McKay stood. "What time was that?"

"I was dressed and already had breakfast made by eight."

"You remember the time?" I asked skeptically.

"I do," she told me coldly. "I attended church at nine and then Hank and I had a picnic luncheon."

"Thank you, Mrs. Cardiff. You've been very helpful. I'll contact you if I have any more questions."

I rose and stuffed my notepad back into my handbag. "We're having some trouble locating Barbara. Could we have her address or her telephone number if she has one?"

Ellen's face hardened. "I haven't spoken to Barbara since the autumn of 1941. When Hugh left to join up I thought Barbara would go back to her old self, the way she was before Hugh came into the picture. Her behaviour became less and less acceptable and I just couldn't allow our friendship to continue. I certainly didn't want people to think I was of the same ilk as Barbara. She left university in the spring of '42. I did hear from one of our girl-friends that she married an Italian who sells meat or something in Little Italy. He's probably a fascist who can't even speak English." She shook her head in disgust.

Like a proper host, Ellen escorted us to the front door which she closed firmly behind us as soon as my feet hit the cement front step.

I managed to hold my tongue until we got into the car. "I hate women like Ellen Cardiff."

"She's certainly judgmental and I don't care for her attitude regarding Italians and Negroes but she's not entirely wrong about Barbara. It seems like she was just trying to look out for her friend, keep her out of trouble and protect her reputation," McKay said.

"Barbara Fisher's reputation doesn't need to be protected. She wasn't doing anything wrong," I told him angrily. "She was young and wanted to experience life. She had a few drinks, stayed out late and listened to jazz music. She wasn't going around robbing and murdering."

McKay smirked. "I think she was doing a little more than staying out late and listening to music."

"And if she was?"

He shifted uncomfortably in his seat. "All I know is that a nice girl doesn't do those things."

"What about a nice boy? Does a nice boy do those things?" I said flippantly. "Were you a nice boy when you were on leave during the war?"

McKay reddened and looked out the window. "Miss Badger, it's just the way things are."

I started the ignition and put the car in gear. "Well, I hate the way things are."

Four

Someone flapped their lips and told the Chief that I went with McKay to interview Ellen Cardiff. I knew right away that it was Stewart from the pompous little smile on his ugly possum-like face. Bertie was not happy with me and I got an earful when I returned to work on Wednesday morning.

"You," he pointed at me. "File, answer the phone and do what Wagner tells you to do." He pointed at McKay. "You. Figure out where young Adams is and be done with it. I can't have you wasting time with this nonsense when we have hundreds of tourists on any given week making trouble." Bertie stalked back into his office and slammed the door.

I leaned up against a filing cabinet. "Is it possible that Adams started towards home but in his drunkenness fell into the lake, hit his head on a rock and drowned?"

McKay put down his pencil and leaned back in his chair. "Every summer there are always two or three drownings. We always find the bodies, even if it's a few days later. Dead bodies float, sooner or later. Besides, if he fell in he would have been close to shore and likely found the next day. And your theory doesn't explain the postcards or how Adams' car ended up in the parking lot of the train station."

Wagner looked up from his typewriter. "I see you're taking the Chief's orders to heart, Miss Badger."

I ignored him. "Alright, then. What if Adams was tied up and weighted down with something? Maybe someone killed him and put his body in a boat, rowed into the middle of the lake and dumped him."

Wagner laughed. "Why? And who?"

"Ellen Cardiff isn't even a hundred pounds; there's no way she could have done it. Bill had already returned to Toronto by that time. Unless Barbara Fisher is an extremely large and muscular woman capable of lifting one hundred and eighty pounds, I don't think that theory holds up," McKay told me.

"One hundred and eighty pounds of dead weight," Wagner added. "You ever try to carry dead weight?"

"What if it wasn't Bill, Ellen or Barbara? What if it was someone else?" I suggested.

McKay laughed. "Miss Badger, you need to stop with these cockamamie theories."

"Are you positive that Bill left town?" I asked.

"Mrs. Cardiff and Mr. and Mrs. Adams all say that he left for basic training before Hugh disappeared but I'll question him. His mother called the station yesterday and talked to Boucher. She gave an address for a rooming house on Sackville Street in Toronto but there's no telephone."

"A rooming house on Sackville?"

"That's what Boucher wrote down," McKay said. "Why?"

"That's a pretty rough area. Poor to lower working class, a fair amount of crime and vice. It just seems like an odd place for a man like Bill Llewellyn to live."

"The Chief wants me to interview him. I doubt he'll be of any help but Bertie wants to make sure I cross my 't's and dot my 'i's. The Chief has confirmed with all branches of the military that even though there are fourteen other men named Hugh

Adams who enlisted and served, none of them is our man. If Adams enlisted he did so using someone else's identification. He may be alive or he may have been killed in action but it's impossible to know unless we can figure out what name he used to enlist," McKay said.

"There might be something to that," I conceded. "He certainly seemed at odds with his parents during that time. Perhaps he didn't want to continue on the path he was on so he assumed another identity." I shook my head. "But then why send the postcards?"

"No matter how troubled your family life is, your family is all you think about when the bullets start whizzing past your head," McKay told me.

"That certainly is true," Wagner said.

"I'll go through the files from the summer of 1941 and look for reports about a missing wallet or stolen identification," I offered.

The big brick house on Albany Avenue in Toronto was my responsibility now and even though I'd installed myself at the cottage in O'Halleran Bay for the spring and summer, I still had to check on the old girl periodically. Plus, I didn't quite trust the neighbourhood boy to cut the grass every week like he said he would. He made me pay him in advance.

The second weekend I was scheduled to work it rained, hot, humid torrential rain that started on Thursday evening and by Friday at noon still hadn't let up. I made big cow eyes at Bertie and sighed sadly and dramatically until he agreed to call in McGinnis so I could have Saturday off. I had just grabbed my umbrella and fastened my hat with an extra pin when Bertie's office door swung open and he yelled for me. A sullen McKay sat in a chair across from the Chief's desk.

"You're going to Toronto today, aren't you?" he asked.

I nodded. "I'm leaving right after I'm done here."

"Perfect," he concluded, slapping his desk. "McKay, you ride with Miss Badger. Get yourself down to Toronto, talk to Bill Llewellyn and go through Adams' bedroom. Mr. Adams has told their housekeeper to expect you. That'll save the city the expense of the train fare."

That damn Albert Parsons. I should have known he wouldn't be moved by cow eyes and a few strategically timed sighs.

"When are you coming back?" he asked me.

"Early Sunday evening," I answered.

The Chief nodded and looked at McKay. "I'll bring Stewart in on Sunday to cover your shift. You catch a ride back with Miss Badger. There now, I've just saved the city the return fare too."

"I'm sure the city can pry open the coffers and find enough for a train ticket," McKay objected.

"No need. You'll catch a ride with Miss Badger. You won't mind the company, will you, Miss Badger? And McKay can take over the driving when it gets to be too much for you." Bertie stood, very pleased that he'd saved the town four dollars. "It's almost noon which means Mrs. Parsons should have my dinner on the table by the time I get home."

He collected his hat from the hook beside the door and plodded out into the main room of the station and out the back door.

"You're not driving my car," I warned him.

"I wouldn't dream of it," McKay answered.

The drive was slower than usual and we arrived in Toronto just in time for McKay's meeting with Bill Llewellyn. McKay had arranged to meet him at a bar on Sackville Street called the Archway Tavern. Don't bother looking for it; it's not there anymore. They tore it down in the '60s and it's a parking lot now. In 1946 the Archway Tavern was a dive that served cheap beer and poor quality liquor to the destitute. I drove down Sackville towards Lake Ontario, passed Queen Street and found the Archway Tavern in the basement level of a red brick building, the blue paint on its sign peeling and the front door slightly ajar. I pulled the Ford into a parking spot across the street.

There was no question of joining McKay to interview Llewellyn. Back in those days bars were only beginning to admit women. The better pubs and bars allowed women to enter with a male escort (never alone) through a separate entrance. Women had to stay with their male escort on one side of the bar and single male patrons stayed on the other side. The Archway Tavern didn't have a separate entrance for women and escorts and even if they had I knew enough to stay out of that place.

McKay got back in the car twenty minutes later, silent and deep in thought.

"It's shellshock, isn't it?" I asked. That's what we called it back then, not that it was something we ever talked about. Now the shrinks call it PTSD. "How bad is it?"

McKay sighed and looked out the window. "It's bad. He can't sleep. He can't work. Loud noises startle him. He drinks and keeps drinking until he passes out but then the nightmares come."

"Was he able to give you any useful information?"

"He remembers the trip to O'Halleran Bay and he remembers why he left early. He was called up and had to report for basic training at Base Borden on July 19th. He left O'Halleran Bay on the 17th. He says he didn't even know Adams enlisted until he came back to Canada in 1944 and his mother told him."

"Do you believe him?"

"It should be easy enough to check but I do believe him."

"Did he give you any more information about Ellen and Barbara?"

"Not much. He thought Barbara was a swell gal but he couldn't stand Ellen. He thought she acted like she was better than everyone else. He agreed that Adams wasn't serious about Barbara but he also said he didn't think Barbara was serious about Adams." McKay turned towards me in his seat. "He said there was definitely something bothering Adams but he didn't know what. Llewellyn said it started around November of 1940. Adams seemed angry but also more critical of everyone and everything. He was less concerned about his classes. His grades dropped and he began missing a few classes here and there. He began drinking a lot and talking non-stop about the war and joining up. He said his father's money was keeping him safe while everybody else was being thrown into the fray. Llewellyn also mentioned that Adams began to talk endlessly about lies and liars."

"That's what Ellen said he was yelling about the night he disappeared," I said. "What lies? And who was lying?"

"Llewellyn doesn't know. If Adams had someone specific in mind, he never said."

"Do you think Llewellyn could have sent the postcards?"

"Why? What possible motive could he have for doing that?"

"Unless," I paused, thinking it through. "What if Adams didn't enlist but just ran away and started a new life? Maybe Llewellyn helped him by sending the postcards to create the illusion that Adams had enlisted."

"He genuinely looked surprised when I told him Adams hadn't enlisted and was instead missing."

I snorted. "Anyone can look surprised. Appearances can be deceiving."

McKay smiled. "Like you, for instance."

"I beg your pardon?"

"You tell me you were a CWAC stationed at military headquarters in London. You tell me you were a stenographer. You tell me this with a look of complete believability on your face. But your shorthand stinks and you have to say the alphabet from A to Z under your breath when you're filing."

"I never said I was a good stenographer," I told him, looking down at the ignition and turning on the car.

"There are so many things we did during the war we can never talk about," McKay said quietly. "I'll never ask you to tell your secrets if you don't ask me to tell mine."

Five

After I dropped McKay at the Y.M.C.A., (Bertie had been kind enough to shell out a dollar a night for a room) I returned to my childhood home on Albany Avenue. I wish you could have seen the house as it was then. I drove by it a few years ago and the beautiful maple in the front yard was gone and its trim was painted a mustard yellow. Mustard yellow on a red brick house. Jesus Christ, it looked like a hamburger. When my family owned it, it had white trim and a black roof and four large dormers with big double-paned windows in the attic. It was a massive house; six bedrooms, a formal dining room and sitting room, a den and a front and back staircase. The kitchen, pantry and informal dining area took up the back quarter of the house. Of course, it only had one bathroom which would be unacceptable now. People need more rooms to shit in than to sleep in these days.

I collected the few pieces of mail that hadn't been forwarded to me at the cottage and carried in the bag of groceries that I'd brought from O'Halleran Bay. Before going to bed I opened up all of the windows to air out the stale, empty feeling that never seemed to leave the old house in those days. It was a house without a family, without people coming and going, cooking and fighting, moving and living. Even though it broke my heart I knew that eventually I would have to sell it.

McKay had agreed to come for breakfast and at eight the next morning a taxicab drove into the driveway and he got out, glancing about uncertainly in the middle of the driveway. I was standing in front of the stove, cooking eggs when I heard the car pull up so I unlatched the window and told him to come around back to the kitchen door. His suit jacket in hand, he came into the kitchen and took off his hat.

"The bacon's done," I gestured to the table. "I hope fried eggs are alright."

"That's fine. Thank you."

"Would you mind putting the toast down? I just know if I leave these eggs for a second I'll ruin them. This stove burns either too hot or not hot enough.

Today it's too hot. There's a coat rack behind the door."

He nodded and pushed down the button on the toaster. "This is all very domestic of you, Miss Badger," he said, hanging up his hat and coat. I made a face. "I don't mean any offence. It's just that I never pictured you cooking."

I slipped the eggs onto a large plate. "Just what exactly did you picture me doing, Corporal McKay?"

He cleared his throat and sat down. "I just didn't think you were the type who took much interest in the domestic arts."

"I'll have you know I'm an excellent cook. Our housekeeper, Mrs. Schmidt, taught me." I put the eggs down on the small kitchen table. Opening the stove, I grabbed the bacon and while I was walking by, the toast popped up. I put it on a plate and set everything down on the table. I took my usual seat near the window and McKay took the chair across from me. "Help yourself."

"A housekeeper? I don't think I've ever met anyone with a housekeeper," McKay said. He took a piece of toast, buttered it and cut it into four strips.

"My mother was ill for many years before she died. My father hired Mrs. Schmidt to take care of us. She moved into the attic and lived here until Dad died."

McKay took a bite of his eggs. "These are good."

"Don't sound so surprised." I stood up to get the coffee pot. I poured two cups and placed one in front of him. "It's quite difficult to ruin eggs."

"Unless you're a cook in the army."

"So I've heard."

"You were a CWAC. You didn't eat at the mess hall?"

I shook my head and buttered my toast. "No. We were organized a little differently than the regular army."

"I wondered about that. You said your flatmate loved his coffee so strong he could stand a spoon in it."

I smiled. "That is what I said."

"His coffee."

"His coffee," I repeated.

"CWACs must have done things differently than the regular army because I can tell you I didn't get to share the barracks with any females. If I had, I think I'd still be in the army."

"You would have if you were married," I told him.

"You're married?" he asked, incredulous.

"I was."

"And now you are..."

76

"Not married," I finished.

He set down his coffee cup and looked at me. "You probably won't believe this but you're the first person I've ever met who's divorced."

"Divorces aren't just for Hollywood couples, you know."

"How long were you married?"

"Six months."

"That's war for you. People get married on the spur of the moment, without really thinking about it. I've seen it dozens of times. Then they regret it and it's splitsville."

"I don't regret my marriage. I still love James very much and I believe he loves me, in his own way. What I regret is that I couldn't be his type."

"His type? What was his type?" McKay asked, popping a whole strip of bacon into his mouth.

I paused, a bit unsure whether I should answer him honestly but then I figured, what the Hell. "You," I answered.

He stopped chewing and stared, trying to figure out if I was having a bit of fun at his expense. Several moments went by before he nodded. "That's a good reason to ask for a divorce."

"I didn't divorce James because he is a homosexual. I divorced him because he lied to me and I couldn't forgive him for that. If he'd just told me from the beginning, been honest from the get-go, I think we'd still be married."

"Really? It didn't bother you? That he..." McKay trailed off.

I smiled. "James is a brilliant scientist, clever and witty. He's interesting and fun to be around, not to mention very handsome. The two of us could have had a nice life together."

"What about children?" McKay asked.

"We were on the same page about that, at least. There was an incident during the war and now," I forced a smile, "children just aren't possible."

It took me a long time to talk about "the incident", partly because back in those days we didn't go around talking about private things the way people do today, airing our secrets and putting pictures of our lady bits all over television. But I also didn't talk about it because I couldn't. I made a vow to my country and my King and I signed an oath agreeing to fifty years of silence about my activities during the war and that vow meant everything to me. It was years before I would tell McKay all the pathetic details about the night Wernher von Baumann, German nephew to one of Churchill's cabinet ministers and a suspected Nazi sympathizer, pushed me down a flight of stairs, kicked the shit out of me and performed the beginnings of a hysterectomy when he stabbed me five times in the torso and pelvis.

"I'm sorry," he said.

I waved a hand. "It's in the past. What about you? Ever been married?"

"No," He shook his head and then looked away.

"But you've been close."

"I used to go with a girl in high school. I was overseas for about a year and she ended it."

"A Dear John letter. That's rough," I told him.

"She's married now."

"This talk has all of a sudden turned dreary and I, for one, have had enough of dreariness. Let's talk about something else." I fished a folded piece of paper out of the pocket of my apron and passed it to him. "I started looking for Barbara Fisher this morning. Assuming Ellen's information is correct and Barbara is living in Little Italy, I think I've narrowed it down to seven men who are possible husbands. That is, of course, assuming she's still in Toronto."

"Alfonso Calderisi, Antonio Cianciolo, Francesco Dal Bello, Attilio Di Meo, Giovanni Folino, Rocco Gagliacco, Emilio Barbaro," McKay read, stumbling through the names in his English Canadian accent.

"I hope to Hell it's not Emilio," I said.

"Why?"

"Because then her name would be Barbara Barbaro."

He put the list down and shook his head. "How did you come up with these names?"

I took a cigarette out of the pack sitting on the table and lit it. "I searched this year's telephone directory and made a list of all of the butcher shops in Little Italy and cross-referenced the names of the owners to determine who lived above their business. It's a start, anyway. The directory only lists the owner of the shop. Barbara's husband may only work at the shop and not own it. He may not work in a shop at all. Ellen might have been just talking out of her ass."

"Very impressive, Miss Badger. If this doesn't lead me to Barbara Fisher it may lead me to someone who knows her." McKay looked at the list again. "These men probably all speak English, right?"

I laughed. "Penso che la vera domanda sia: ti parleranno?" I think the real question is: Will they speak to you?

Poor McKay. He was so wholesome, so thoroughly Canadian that he didn't have a clue. Don't get me wrong. I'm not saying he was stupid; he was exceptionally smart, an excellent policeman and investigator. You had to be in those days; it's not like today. You couldn't just run DNA through a machine and identify your killer. There was no DNA, no internet, no videos, no cell phones. Most of the time there wasn't even any backup if you got into trouble. You had to be tough as nails, a thinker, you had to actually put clues together, with nothing more than really good detective work and your gut. And McKay was a genius at all of that but he wasn't worldly. It wasn't that he was naive. He just couldn't conceive of anything other than his little town full of people who looked like him and for the most part had the same life experiences as he'd had. Oh, he'd been to Europe but that had been as a soldier. He couldn't imagine a situation where someone wouldn't trust the police and wouldn't offer to tell them everything they knew.

"Let me do the talking," McKay told me as we walked along College Street. "I'll talk and if I need you to translate, I'll ask."

We stopped in front of a little shop and McKay checked my list. "This should be Giovanni Folino."

A bell tinkled above the door as we walked into the butcher shop. Different meats hung on strings around the small store and behind the glass display case was a man who looked to be about fifty. He smiled when he saw us.

"Good day, sir and madam. What I get for you?" he asked in heavily accented English.

"Giovanni Folino?" McKay asked.

I saw his eyes briefly register panic. He smiled and shook his head. "No."

"You're not Giovanni Folino?" McKay asked suspiciously.

"No. No person here," the man said, still smiling.

"Do you know where I might find Mr. Folino?" McKay asked.

"No."

I stepped forward. "Mi scusi signore. Perdonate il mio terribile accento italiano. Sto cercando di aiutare questo signore qui. Sta cercando di trovare una donna che crediamo sia sposata con un macellaio o un proprietario di un negozio in questa zona. È una donna canadese. Si chiama Barbara Fisher."

He didn't say anything for a long time and I was worried that perhaps my Italian was worse than I thought it was. Finally, he glanced over at McKay. "Polizia?" he asked me.

I nodded but held up my hands when I saw a worried look cross his face. "Corporal McKay is not here to arrest anyone. A friend of Barbara's is missing and may be in danger. Corporal McKay just wants to know if Barbara can help us find her friend. Please. No one is in trouble, I promise you," I said in Italian.

"Non conosco questa Barbara Fisher," he answered.

"What did he say?" McKay asked.

"He said he doesn't know anyone named Barbara Fisher," I grinned at the man, took a step closer and leaned on the display case. "This is the biggest shop within two blocks. Sai tutto quello che succede da queste parti. Chi ha un figlio da queste parti che ha sposato una ragazza canadese?"

He sighed and looked uneasy. It was hard for him to talk to the police and I respected that.

"A young man is missing and his family wants to find him. His mother is heartbroken. Sua madre ha il cuore spezzato. Corporal McKay wants to help. Please," I begged.

"Rocco Gagliacco. Il figlio," he told me finally.

I smiled. "Thank you." Turning to McKay, I explained. "He says Gagliacco's son, also named Rocco."

"You speak not so bad," he told me.

"That's high praise indeed, coming from a native speaker. Thank you," I said in Italian.

We turned to go. The man made a noise and came around the counter after us. He placed one hand on my arm and with the other reached into his pants pocket. He withdrew a small photograph, its corners bent and several creases marking the shiny surface. A young man in an Italian army uniform smiled at us.

"Mio figlio," he said.

I smiled. "Your son is very handsome. Bello. Molto bello."

"You should be real proud of him," McKay added.

The man put the photograph back into his pocket and patted my arm. "Artbroken," he said slowly in English before returning to his place behind the counter.

Rocco Gagliacco Senior had a small delicatessen three blocks west on College Street. We walked along, trying to stay in the shade of the store awnings to hide from the unseasonably warm spring sun.

"Where did you learn to speak Italian like that?"

"I studied modern languages at university," I reminded him. "Mr. Folino is very kind. My accent isn't very good. My professor always told me I sounded like a German who spoke French and was trying to read Italian. You were in Italy. You didn't pick up any Italian while you were there?"

"I tried to say something once but I must have mispronounced some words because a lady slapped my face," McKay said.

"I've never been to Italy. Maybe in a few years, once the world has settled down a bit I'll be able to go."

"It's beautiful. Even in wartime, I could tell it was beautiful."

I stopped abruptly in front of a large, colourful sign nailed to a post. "Lichee Garden Restaurant and Club. Famous Chinese Food. Elegant dining room. Open 11 am to 5 am daily. Band plays nightly," I read. "It looks beautiful. My goodness, it even has a license to serve liquor."

McKay eyed it critically. "What sort of food do you think Chinese people eat?"

"Rice, for one."

"I've never had that. You?"

"Once or twice. Sometimes my father's patients would give him food to thank him. But that was a long time ago before he became a surgeon and before Mrs. Schmidt. After she came we ate a lot of German food."

"You speak German?"

"I'm fluent in English, French and German and passable in Italian and Spanish."

"German. That must have made you pretty useful during the war."

Ignoring him, I looked up and pointed to a red sign. "This is it."

We entered and a short, thin man stood behind the counter, a white apron around his middle. He was young and very attractive and he smiled at us when we entered.

"Good morning, Sir, Miss."

"Are you Rocco Gagliacco?" McKay asked.

He hesitated then nodded curtly, all friendliness gone. "I am."

"I'm Corporal Joe McKay with the O'Halleran Bay police force. I'm looking for a woman by the name of Barbara Fisher."

He shrugged. "Don't know her."

"Please. She's not in trouble. Per favore. Non è nei guai. One of her old friends is missing; a man named Hugh Adams. Hugh Adams è scomparso. Ci chiediamo se lei sa dov'è."

"I'm not here to arrest your wife, Mr. Gagliacco. I just want to talk about her friend, Hugh Adams," McKay assured him.

"I haven't heard from Hugh in years." A petite brunette, her hair held back in a blue scarf and one hand resting on her large, pregnant belly stood in a doorway behind the counter of the small shop. "I was Barbara Fisher. I'm Barbara Gagliacco now."

"Is there somewhere we could talk?" I asked, eyeing her husband. I wasn't sure Barbara wanted him to hear about her relationship with another man. "You look like you could sit down for a bit."

"We can go upstairs," she offered. Her husband made a move to protest but she put her hand on his arm, squeezed it and smiled. We followed her through the doorway to a narrow hallway and up a flight of steep stairs to the apartment above. The apartment was bright and everything in it had a newness to it, as if it had just come off the Eaton's truck. She sat down in a chair and put her feet up on a stool. "My husband wasn't trying to lie to you, Constable. He is distrustful of the police and the government. You see, he was declared a person of suspicion in 1941 and put into an internment camp."

"I understand, Mrs. Gagliacco. And it's Corporal, Corporal Joe McKay," he corrected her. "I'm look- ing into the disappearance of Hugh Adams and I was hoping to get some information from you.

"Disappearance?" she said.

"His parents originally thought he ran away to enlist but after the war when he didn't come home they contacted the Department of Defense.

There's no record that he ever enlisted. Mr. and Mrs. Adams now believe that he's missing and has been missing since 1941."

She sat up and furrowed her brow. "I can't believe it. I was so sure he'd enlisted. It was all he'd been talking about for months. I was so happy he finally had the nerve to do it."

"Do you remember the last time you saw Hugh?" McKay asked.

"Of course. We had dinner at his parents' summer home then went to a dance at one of the lodges. Afterwards, we went for some drinks."

"I think you had more than a few drinks," McKay said.

"I'm sure we did. We probably had too many," she told him. "We went to a little tavern outside of town. I can't remember the name but there was a band and it had a large covered porch at the front."

McKay nodded. "I know the place you're talking about. How would you describe Hugh's mood that evening?"

"It started out fine. We were having a lot of fun but as the evening went on and Hugh had more and more to drink he turned foul. He was angry and combative. I demanded he take me back to the cottage."

"And once you got to the cottage?"

Barbara thought. "I guess I just went to bed. When Hugh got like that I usually just left him alone."

"Was that the last time you saw him?" McKay asked.

"Yes. I remember hearing his car pulling out of the driveway some time later. I can't be sure of the exact time, though."

"What happened the next morning?"

"I woke up but Ellen was already gone. She went to church services and then on a picnic with a young man, Hank, whom she'd met the previous week. I don't recall his last name but I think Ellen ended up marrying him."

"Did Hugh get angry often?" I asked.

"No. I mean, not usually, not in the beginning. When we first started going together he was so much fun. He drank, perhaps too much, but he was never angry or vicious. He was a gas," Barbara said.

"When did that change?" McKay asked.

"It had been about a year. Hugh wanted to enlist but his father had convinced him to wait until after he finished law school. He was starting his last year but his father was doing everything he could to keep him out of the service. Hugh had a strong sense of right and wrong. Most people don't know that about him. He wanted to be a lawyer because he thought he could help people. When he found out about what was going on in Europe he was enraged by the injustice of it. He told me once that if he didn't enlist then he was condoning everything that the Nazis and Mussolini were doing. That was initially why he contacted Joshua Lipowicz, to see how he could help."

"Who's Joshua Lipowicz?" McKay asked, writing the name down in his notebook.

"Mr. and Mrs. Adams didn't mention anyone by that name," I told her.

Barbara rolled her eyes. "I'm not surprised. Lipowicz is a lawyer. Hugh met him when he came to the university looking for law students to volunteer at his office. He provides free legal services, mostly to the poor and new immigrants so Mr. Adams and his cronies don't have many good things to say about Lipowicz. You see, Mr. Adams never did anything for free."

"Did Hugh work for Lipowicz?"

Barbara nodded. "He volunteered every Friday. We both did. In fact, I worked at the office until a few months ago when I stopped being able to see my feet. Most of the work doesn't require a lawyer. Most people just can't read or write in English well enough to fill out forms or respond to government letters. Lipowicz is one of the lawyers helping Toronto Jews bring remaining family members to Canada and corresponding with the Red Cross on behalf of families who are still looking for their relatives. During the war, he was instrumental in getting more than two hundred Italian men released from internment camps. That's how I met my husband."

"Do you know if Hugh intended to continue working for Lipowicz?"

"You'd have to check with him to be sure but I understood that was Hugh's plan."

"Did Mr. Adams know that Hugh was not planning to join his law firm?" McKay asked.

"Mr. Adams knew that Hugh wanted to work for Lipowicz but he didn't accept it. He chalked it up to one of Hugh's fanciful ideas," Barbara said.

"Where's Mr. Lipowicz's office?" McKay asked.

"On Palmerston. He's closed today but he'll be there tomorrow. The office is closed, of course, but he'll be there doing paperwork."

"On Sunday?" McKay asked, incredulous.

"The Jewish holy day is today," I told McKay. I turned to Barbara. "There's one thing I don't understand. Hugh was a grown man. He didn't need anyone's permission to enlist. Why didn't he just do it if he felt that strongly?" I asked.

"Hugh wanted to enlist in 1939 when Canada declared war but at that time he valued his father's opinion, really respected and looked up to him. Mr. Adams convinced him to wait and finish his education. He told Hugh that he would make a greater difference, be a more effective officer, if he went in with more maturity and life experience under his belt. But as the war went on, Hugh came to see his education as less and less important. He wanted to do his part. I noticed in the last year or so before Hugh left that he'd been more and more critical of his father. They hadn't been getting along very well. That's why, when Hugh disappeared, I thought he'd finally gone and done it. And honestly, I was glad he was getting away from his old man."

"What do you mean by that?" I asked.

Barbara shifted uncomfortably in her chair. "One afternoon I was coming out of a class when I was stopped by Hugh's father. He said he was at the university meeting a friend and thought he'd take the opportunity to meet me. At that point, I wasn't even aware that Hugh's family knew about me. He said he'd walk with me on my way to McKinley Hall. Mr. Adams told me that Hugh was more determined than ever about enlisting but that I could help keep Hugh in Canada and away from the war. I told him I didn't know how in the world I could do that. Mr. Adams said that if Hugh was a father he might be persuaded to give up the idea of enlisting because he would have family obligations. Then in the next breath, he assured me that he'd make sure Hugh married me and that I was well taken care of. I was shocked and thoroughly embarrassed. I never told Hugh until his mother called to invite me to O'Halleran Bay. I was going to decline the invitation but my friend, Ellen Hale, suggested going up as a group so his father wouldn't get the wrong idea."

"So it was Ellen's idea to accompany you?" McKay clarified.

"Yes. As I said, I was all set to decline the invitation until Ellen turned it into a group holiday. Hugh rented the cottage for Ellen and me. I couldn't bear to be under the same roof as Mr. Adams."

"We were under the impression that Ellen didn't like Hugh. Did it seem strange to you that she suggested both of you go to O'Halleran Bay?" I said.

"Ellen and Hugh couldn't stand each other," Barbara laughed. "But she was willing to put up with him if it meant rubbing elbows with people like the Adamses. I suspect she had ulterior motives when she suggested the trip to O'Halleran Bay."

"What were those ulterior motives, Mrs. Gagliacco?" McKay asked.

Barbara laughed. "Ellen didn't really want to become a teacher. She accepted the university scholarship for the sole purpose of finding a husband.

And not just any husband. Ellen wanted a man from a good family with money or, at the very least, prospects. Initially, she was pleased when I started going with Hugh because she thought she could ingratiate herself into his group of friends and attract someone's interest. Poor Ellen. She always tried so hard and put on airs. It was off-putting. I'm sure she suggested going with me to O'Halleran Bay because she saw it as an opportunity to meet some of the wealthy young men who were summering there with their families." Barbara shifted uncomfortably in her chair. She tucked a pillow behind her back. "Growing up, Ellen and I both lived in the same tenement. Paper-thin walls, no running water, no electricity, families of ten crowded into three rooms. My family was poor but at least there was always food on the table. Ellen wasn't so lucky. There were twelve children in her family. Her father, like mine, worked at a brick factory but unlike mine drank away most of his wages. She had no intention of going back to Corktown."

"Bill Llewellyn said that something seemed to be bothering Hugh as far back as the autumn of 1940. Do you have any idea what that might have been?" McKay asked.

Barbara thought for a moment then nodded. "I think Bill's correct. That's when Hugh started to drink a lot more." She paused. "I don't know if this means anything but something odd happened in December 1940. The University of Toronto's Snow Ball was set for the beginning of December."

"Snowball?" McKay asked.

"No. The Snow Ball. It's the annual winter formal dance," I explained to McKay.

"Hugh and I had arranged to go together in October. I remember because I bought my dress on Thanksgiving weekend during the Simpson's sale. Five days before the dance Hugh said he had other plans and couldn't go. I was furious with him and, in fact, I refused to see him or take his calls during the Christmas holidays and for most of January."

"Do you know what his plans were?" I asked.

"He wouldn't tell me and I found that strange because Hugh wasn't usually secretive. He called me late on the Sunday after the Snow Ball but I wouldn't take his calls. Ellen said he was with another woman but I think she just said that; I don't think she had any proof."

"Thank you Mrs. Gagliacco. You've been very helpful," McKay told her.

Barbara struggled to stand up.

"Don't get up. Stay off your feet for a while. We can let ourselves out," I told her.

"Hugh is very special to me, Corporal. When I met him my whole world opened up and I'll always be very grateful for that," Barbara said. "When you find him, please let him know I wish him well."

After we met with Barbara, I drove north on Yonge Street and went east to the Rosedale area of Toronto. The same words I used to describe it then still apply now: money, money, money. The Adams house was a massive brick structure with a gigantic bevelled front window on the bottom floor, and a front porch with thick columns, styled after ancient Greek architecture. The second floor housed a small wrought iron balcony and large windows. Two large dormers with wide windows, several of them open in the late spring sun, stuck out of the third-floor attic.

"Adams must be a very good lawyer or represent some very bad people," I said as I brought the Ford to a stop in the circular driveway.

"He's a lawyer at Burnham and Bolt," McKay responded.

"That sounds like a law firm right out of The Three Stooges."

The front door was opened by a housekeeper dressed in a neat, black uniform. She was expecting McKay but eyed me suspiciously, even after he introduced me as the police force's stenographer.

"This way please." She led us brusquely up the wide stairs to the second floor and stopped in front of a closed door. "This is Hugh's room. I understand that you plan to look around but please put everything back exactly as it is. When you're done please ring the bell on the table," she pointed to a little brass bell sitting on a half-moon table in the hallway, "and I will escort you out."

"Thank you," McKay told her but she was already halfway down the hallway.

The room felt abandoned like nothing had been touched in it for a long time even though the bed was made and there wasn't a spec of dust anywhere. A large built-in bookshelf and desk took up one wall. Beside the bed, there was a tall dresser. On the wall opposite the bookshelf were two closed doors. McKay opened one cautiously to reveal a closet, almost empty of clothes except for a few suits in laundry bags and a collection of miscellaneous sports equipment. He opened the second door and peered inside.

"Would you get a load of this?" he said, pushing open the door wide to reveal a white tiled floor.

"A bathroom?" I peeked inside. "He has his own bathroom?"

"The life of the rich," McKay said. He looked around. "I'm going to go through the desk. Sit down on the bed and don't touch anything."

I sighed and sat down on the bed. While he was going through the desk, I scooted over to the dresser and looked through the drawers. They were almost empty and held nothing of interest. I stood up and looked under the bed. Not even a dust bunny. Undaunted, I lifted the mattress and felt around.

"What are you doing?" McKay asked.

My hand clasped some paper and I withdrew what passed for a naughty magazine in the 1940s. My God, how tame those magazines were compared to the ones today. I think at that time the pin-up girls still wore clothes. I flipped through it and showed McKay one of the pictures. "Poor girl. She'll get frostbite frolicking around like that in the snow, don't you think?"

He reddened slightly, grabbed the magazine from me and shoved it back under the mattress. I moved to a collection of textbooks on the bookshelf and flipped through one, noticing the notes in the margins.

"We should take one of these so we can compare the writing on the postcards to Hugh's writing," I said. I squinted at the scrawls in the margins. "He certainly won't be winning any prizes for his penmanship, that's for certain."

"*We* will not be comparing anything. I will be. And the chief, if necessary."

I ignored him and continued to flip through the books on the shelf. Two identical bound black leather books caught my eye. I pulled the first one out and leafed through it.

"McKay, take a look at this."

He looked over my shoulder. "What is that?"

"It's Adams' appointment book from 1940," I told him. I looked at the other volume. "And 1941. He listed all of his classes, assignments, and university events. There are a few phone numbers and some random notations scattered throughout. Adams seems to have liked jazz and blues music. He has concert times and places written down on most weekends." I flipped forward to a large calendar showing the month of December and pointed to the note on the seventh. "He made note of the Snow Ball but then crossed it out in a different coloured ink. It looks like Barbara was right. He planned to go but changed his mind at some point." I skipped forward in the book to the page dedicated to the seventh of December. "He has a whole bunch of notes and appointments to do with the Snow Ball but they're all crossed out." I pointed to a notation hastily written in pencil at the bottom of the page. "GREYSTOCK 3 11," I read.

"Greystock," McKay repeated. "It could be an address."

"I've never heard of a Greystock street in Toronto," I said. "But I suppose it's possible. I don't know every street and I'm not familiar with the suburban areas."

"I don't know a town called Greystock, at least not in Ontario," McKay said.

"Maybe it's someone's last name?" I took the two appointment books and shoved them into my handbag.

McKay went back to searching the desk and I went back to the bookshelf. An examination of the dresser drawers yielded nothing useful so we rang the little brass bell and were escorted down the stairs by the housekeeper. After we were shown to the front entrance, the heavy oak door was shut firmly in our faces.

Six

Sundays used to be different. Isn't it funny that a whole day can change in the span of a lifetime? Everything was closed on Sundays and people were expected to attend church whether they felt like it or believed a damn thing the minister was saying. Sundays were a break from work, for socializing and going to big family dinners. Even those who didn't give a rat's ass end about God or convention knew enough not to mow their lawn on Sunday. Of course, now that I say this I realize that this was only *my* experience at the time and there was a whole other Toronto out there, one that didn't rest on Sundays.

I spent that Sunday morning with a pot of coffee and The Heart is a Lonely Hunter by Carson Mc-

Cullers (didn't care for it, by the way). If my parents had been alive I probably would have dutifully gone to church with them but I'd kind of given up on the whole religion thing since the war. I picked up McKay from the YMCA just after ten and drove to Lipowicz's office on Palmerston Avenue.

The office of Zimmerman, Lipowicz, Romano and De Luca, Barristers and Solicitors, was sandwiched between a kosher deli and a bookstore. Like all of the other stores on the street, Lipowicz's office was closed, the blinds in the front window drawn and the lights off. It didn't matter in those days that the Jewish religion permitted working on Sundays. Everyone was expected to follow the Christian tradition on which Canada had been founded and if you didn't like it, too bad.

McKay pounded loudly on the office door three times before a thin, clean-shaven man wearing a grey suit and gold-rimmed glasses appeared.

"We're closed," the man yelled through the door.

McKay reached into his pocket and pulled out his policeman's I.D. card and badge. "I'm looking for Joshua Lipowicz," McKay yelled back through the glass.

The man unlocked the door and stood aside to allow us entry. "You've found him."

McKay stuck out his hand. "Corporal Joe McKay from the O'Halleran Bay Police Force."

Lipowicz shook his hand. "O'Halleran Bay? Where's that?"

"About three hours north," McKay answered.

"I've broken no Sunday Laws," Lipowicz said.

"I'm not here about the Sunday Laws. I'm here about a man named Hugh Adams."

"There's a name I haven't heard in a few years," Lipowicz said.

"That's the problem," I told him.

"This is Miss Badger, our force's stenographer," McKay said.

Lipowicz glanced outside uneasily. "Come. My office is in the back. I don't want someone to get the wrong idea."

McKay and I followed him to a small unadorned office with a cluttered desk and two wooden chairs set out for clients. I took the one closest to the door.

"Why have you come to me about Adams? It's been years since I've seen him," Lipowicz said.

"His family believes that he's missing and have asked the O'Halleran Bay Police Force to look into it," McKay said as he sat down in the other chair.

"Missing?" Lipowicz sat down at his desk and pushed a pile of papers to the side. "I was told that he enlisted."

"I understand that Hugh Adams worked for you back in 1941 here at your practice," McKay said.

Lipowicz nodded. "My associates and I run a free legal clinic on Fridays. He was a volunteer at the clinic."

"I know it was a few years ago but do you remember the last time you saw him?" McKay asked.

Lipowicz shook his head. "I don't specifically remember the last time I saw him but I do remember learning that he had enlisted and wouldn't be coming to work here."

"It's true, then? Adams was going to work here for you after graduation?" I said.

"He was going to work for the firm, not me specifically. He was going to do his articling here and then once he passed his examinations and was called to the Bar we hoped he would stay on. He was supposed to start at the end of August, only the end of August came and he didn't show up," Lipowicz told us. "I figured he changed his mind and went to work for his father instead so I called the old man up. Our conversation lasted ten seconds. He told me that Hugh enlisted and the next thing I heard was a dial tone in my ear."

"Mr. Adams senior knew that Hugh was supposed to come and work for you?" McKay confirmed.

I looked at McKay but said nothing. He caught my gaze. If that was true then Adams had lied in his initial interview with McKay.

"He knew alright even if he wasn't happy about it."

"He wanted his son to work with him," I said.

"He wanted his son to work with him or with a group of lawyers he approved of," Lipowicz told us.

"And Mr. Adams Senior didn't approve of you, of this firm? Did he lose to you in court once and carry a grudge?" McKay asked.

"No, nothing like that though I assure you that if I met Adams in court he would certainly lose." Seeing my expression, he explained. "That's not a misplaced sense of grandeur, Miss Badger. I'm an excellent court lawyer, and that's why wealthy clients will pay handsomely for my services. Those wealthy clients fund this firm's legal clinic. Adams pushes paper; he deals mostly with real estate transactions and wills. No, it's nothing like that. Neither Adams nor anyone at Burnham and Bolt, care for the heritage of the lawyers here at this firm."

McKay shook his head, confused. "Mr. Lipowicz, you'll have to speak more plainly. What do you mean?"

"I think," I began hesitatingly, "you're saying Mr. Adams and the lawyers at Burnham and Bolt are anti-semites?"

"Yes, among other things. I don't take it personally. They hate Catholics too. And anyone whose skin is darker than their own."

"But Hugh Adams wasn't like his father, was he?" I said.

Lipowicz smiled. "Not in the least. I didn't know him well on a personal level but I can tell you he was very concerned about what was happening in Europe. He believed in democracy and wanted to use the court system to uphold it for everyone, regardless of religion or skin colour. He didn't always get it right but he made an effort to understand different faiths, and ways of living, and people appreciated that. He struck me as intelligent and quick. I thought he would have been an excellent court lawyer because he had the uncanny ability to anticipate what his opposing counsel was going to say and do. I was looking forward to working with him."

"Did Hugh Adams ever attempt to contact you himself? Did you ever receive any letters or postcards from him?"

Lipowicz shook his head. "Never heard from him again."

McKay stood. "Thank you for your time, Mr. Lipowicz. We'll leave you to your Sunday scripture meditations, which is no doubt what you were doing before we interrupted you."

Lipowicz followed us to the door and unlocked it. Just as I was about to pass through the doorway, I stopped and turned to him.

"Does the word 'Greystock' mean anything to you?" I asked.

He thought then shook his head. I followed McKay into the Sunday silence of Palmerston Avenue.

Before finally heading back to O'Halleran Bay, I had a stop to make. It couldn't be helped; I'd already made the arrangements. I crossed the city while McKay sat silently beside me. I pulled off Bayview Avenue just after passing Eglinton and drove down a little lane, coming to a stop beside an immense stone and brick building. Sunnybrook Hospital was just new then and was exclusively a hospital for Canadian veterans.

"My brother, Johnny, is here. I haven't seen him in about a month. Sunday is the only day they allow visits." I explained.

"Was he Army or Air Force?" McKay asked.

107

"Air Force. He flew dozens of missions before he was shot down over Germany. He was picked up by an American patrol a few days later, thank God."

"I'll stay in the car if you like," he offered.

"There's no need unless you want to. Johnny's usually out on the grounds during visiting hours. You can wander around if you like," I said.

Together we walked up the wide stone steps, Canada's coat of arms sitting boldly atop the entrance doors. I signed in at the office and followed the rest of the Sunday visitors outside to the gardens. As I predicted, Johnny was already there, sitting in a wheelchair and covered in a blanket despite the warm weather.

"I'll wander around," McKay told me.

I nodded and started towards Johnny. I called his name and when he looked up I waved. He stared at me blankly for a few seconds before waving back. When I caught up to him, I hugged him, feeling his thin body through his shirt.

"It's so good to see you," I told him. "You're looking well."

"I've missed you, Villy," he smiled.

I gripped the handles on the wheelchair, disengaged the brake and pushed Johnny towards a stone bench. "I'm sorry. It's been a few weeks, hasn't it? I've been up in O'Halleran Bay at the cottage."

"Is Lizzie up there with you? She hasn't been around to see me in a while," he asked.

I swallowed and stubbornly held the tears at bay. "No, Johnny. Lizzie's not with me."

"She's probably busy studying. The nursing programme takes up so much of her time. I keep telling her that she doesn't need to bother. When we get married she won't be working anyway."

I didn't correct him. I didn't tell him that Lizzie hadn't been around to see him a while ago; she'd never been to see him. I didn't tell him that she'd finished the nursing programme four years ago, that she'd moved away and married someone else.

"I'll call her tonight," he told me, smiling.

I set the wheelchair's brake and sat down on the bench. "I'm working for the police force in O'Halleran Bay. It will probably only be until the fall."

"I can't believe you didn't get into university, Villy. Your marks are superior. I hope you're planning to try again. Maybe Dad could ask Mr. Johnson from the hospital to write you a letter of recommendation."

"Maybe."

"Well, I think it's worth a try at least."

"I'll think about it," I promised him.

109

For the next half hour, we talked about everything and nothing. Johnny jumped from one subject to another, twice asking me if I could remind Dad to send him his notes from his biology class because he was sure the exam had to be coming up soon. He wondered when he would be healed enough from his appendectomy to go home and whispered conspiratorially that everyone in his ward was nutty but there hadn't been any other beds available so he was stuck there.

As our visit ended, I noticed McKay waiting patiently in a chair near a fountain and waved him over.

"This is Joe McKay," I told Johnny. "He's a corporal in the O'Halleran Bay Police Force."

Johnny shook his hand but eyed him suspiciously. "Does Dad know about him?" he asked.

"He's a friend, Johnny. I'm giving him a ride back to O'Halleran Bay."

I bent to hug him goodbye and Johnny clung onto me, whispering in my ear: "That's probably a good thing, Villy. He's much too old for you."

I smirked. At that time McKay was three years younger than I was.

Later, in the car, McKay asked me about Johnny's prognosis.

"No one knows. At first, the doctors thought it would only be a matter of a few weeks before he returned to normal but that was almost a year ago."

Johnny was permanently stuck in the past, suspended somewhere between 1935 and 1939, living in a dream, one that had no knowledge of the war. He was lost to me and would never return.

Seven

On Monday just after one o'clock, McKay and MacInnis returned from the library, entered through the back door and plopped into the chairs scattered around the large table in the kitchenette area. McKay threw a stack of books down on the table. I stubbed my cigarette out in the ashtray on McKay's desk and stood up from his chair.

"Why do you two look so down in the mouth? Too many books with too many big words?" I said.

"All that reading for nothing," MacInnis said.

McKay rubbed his eyes. "There's no Greystock town in Ontario. There's no Greystock road, street, avenue, crescent, concession or boulevard in the entire province of Ontario."

"We even checked New York State," MacInnis added.

McKay looked at me quizzically. "What are you still doing here?"

"I was waiting for you. I found something." I held up a piece of paper. "Hugh Adams' car was cream-coloured, correct?"

"Yes. A Chevrolet with a green rear quarter panel," McKay said.

I shoved the paper under his nose. "Look at this police report and look at the date."

McKay scanned the paper. "Sunday, July twentieth, 1941. Ray Armstrong was almost hit on his way to church, just after nine-thirty by a cream-coloured Chev with a green rear panel."

"That means Adams was still in town mid-morning on Sunday," I said.

"Or someone was driving his car," McKay muttered.

MacInnis looked at me, his big blue eyes wide. "Golly, Miss Badger. You're a regular..." he paused, searching for words, "detective."

I should stop here and tell you a little bit about MacInnis. We used to call men like MacInnis "a real dreamboat". He looked a little like a young Burt Lancaster except less rugged and more beautiful. He wasn't old enough then to be handsome; he was still beautiful with a face and a body that looked like it was chiselled out of marble. He could have been a Hollywood movie star. But, dear God, talking to him was like talking to an eight-year-old boy. I suppose it didn't really matter since if you were with him it wasn't for his riveting conversational skills. He had women, young and old, just falling into his lap but he seemed completely oblivious to their intentions. I have to admit that I had half a mind to fall into his lap myself but I couldn't bear the thought of looking into those big, blue vacant eyes.

"I'm glad you found something, Miss Badger, because we found exactly nothing," McKay said.

"Maybe Greystock is a person and not a street," I suggested.

MacInnis, who was standing at the sink and holding the kettle under the faucet, shook his head. "We thought of that. Nothing. No listings in any Ontario directory."

"Alright. What about the numbers? Three and eleven," I said.

"We thought maybe three was the street number and eleven was an apartment or unit number," McKay answered.

"If it's not an address, what else could the numbers be? Three and eleven," I repeated.

"The date?" MacInnis suggested. "The third month is March. Eleven could be the day."

I took Adams' two black leather-bound appointment books from McKay's desk and opened them up. I flipped through the pages until I found March eleventh. "In 1940 on March eleventh Adams wrote about a paper due for Ruttledge, whoever that is. Then there's a list of calculations with a total and the note 'bill for car'."

"What about '41?" McKay asked.

I looked at the other book. "A notation that looks like it was copied from a textbook and then he scribbled a note that says 'Teddy six o'clock, Green Room Jazz Club.' I think. Adams' penmanship is terrible." I looked up from the appointment book. "Maybe it's not March eleventh. Could it be November third?"

McKay sighed. "It could be any of those things. Or none of them."

"If Greystock is a person," I suggested. "Eleven could be a time. Maybe it's a meeting."

"It would either have to be an eleven o'clock meeting three months before Adams disappeared or," MacInnis counted on his fingers, "seven months after. That is if the three represents March."

"We're going around in circles. I'm beginning to think GREYSTOCK 3 11 means nothing," McKay said.

I opened the appointment book back to December seventh, 1940 and examined the page again, reading it through carefully and observing every letter, every notation, every mark Adams had made.

"It's not GREYSTOCK," I said.

"What?" McKay hurried over to his desk and peered down at the page.

I pointed to the letters. "I think it's two words; Grey and Stock. Adams' writing is little more than a scrawl but do you see how the space between the 'y' and the 's' is slightly larger?"

McKay squinted at the letters. "I think you may be right." He looked up at MacInnis. "Leave the teapot, MacInnis. Open the Toronto directory and see if there's a Grey Street or a Stock Street."

"How do you know it's in Toronto?" I asked.

"Mrs. Gagliacco said that Adams was gone Saturday but had returned by Sunday. He couldn't have gone very far."

"Not in December on roads in Ontario," I agreed.

"I found it," MacInnis called out. "Or, rather, them. I found them. There's a Stock Avenue in Etobicoke Township, near Mimico." He flipped to another section of the directory. "There's a Grey Road and also a Gray Avenue. That's 'Gray' using the American spelling."

"Where are they located in the city?" McKay asked.

"It says here Grey Road is in North York and Gray Avenue is in a place called Mount Dennis," MacInnis said.

"Mount Dennis is northwest of downtown, North York is northeast," I told them.

"Do any of those streets list a building at number three or eleven?" McKay asked.

"Grey Road starts at number seventy-eight. That's odd. Why would they start the house numbers at seventy-eight? What happened to all of the other numbers?" MacInnis asked with complete seriousness.

"What about Gray Avenue?" McKay asked.

MacInnis looked at the directory and nodded his head. "It has houses at number three and eleven."

"Check Stock Avenue," I told him.

He flipped pages, glanced down at the book and nodded again. "Yes, ma'am. It sure does."

"Who lives at number three and at number eleven?" I asked.

"It says here George Burnham lives at number three and..."

"Burnham?" I interrupted. "As in Burnham and Bolt?"

"That can't be a coincidence," McKay said.

"It was a meeting. Adams was supposed to meet someone at George Burnham's house," I said.

"Maybe at eleven o'clock," McKay said.

"Maybe someone named Grey," I added.

McKay sighed and sat down at his desk. "I'm beginning to think that Mr. Adams has withheld quite a bit of information that would have been helpful. I'm going to get the Chief to bring him in. Adams might be more forthcoming if Parsons presses him."

The image of Humpty Dumpty chasing Mr. Adams with a billy club sprang into my mind and I couldn't help but laugh uncontrollably.

Eight

I was pleased when McKay knocked on the wooden screen door at the cottage later that evening but not entirely surprised. I'd begged him and even agreed to make his tea at work for a month if he'd tell me everything about the interview with Lawrence Adams. I admit that I flattered myself just a little bit thinking that maybe the chance to see me outside of work hours was more important than a hot cup of tea but, as I said before, it was hard to tell just exactly what McKay was thinking.

I held open the door. "Come in. I was just having a drink. Can I get you one?"

He took off his cap but didn't move. "I shouldn't."

I walked out onto the porch, letting the door swing shut behind me. "Shouldn't come in? Or shouldn't have a drink?"

"O'Halleran Bay is dry," he reminded me.

"I bought this alcohol in Toronto legally and I'm drinking it in my own house on my own property, Corporal. Even you should find that within the confines of the law," I told him. "But I'm sure there's a Coca-Cola kicking around here somewhere if you'd rather."

"And it wouldn't look right if someone saw me going into your house at night."

I laughed. "It's seven o'clock in the evening. Good God, it's still light out. Not to mention, we're almost thirty years old."

"It wouldn't reflect well on you, Miss Badger, if a neighbour saw me going into your house by myself in the evening. O'Halleran Bay is a very small town."

I sighed loudly. "Alright. We'll sit on the porch, in chairs placed ten feet apart and we'll make sure to keep our hands in plain view at all times. Perhaps if you'd had the footman send an engraved invitation I could have scared up a chaperone, an old spinster aunt that I keep in the cellar for just such purposes or a vicar and his homely wife."

McKay smiled wryly and sat down on one of the wooden chairs on the porch. "Are you finished?"

I took a drink and rolled my eyes. "Yes."

"I just came by to let you know that the Adams' case has been closed."

"Closed? By whom? Why?"

"By the Chief. Bertie and I just came from speaking with Mr. Adams. He was not forthcoming at first but Bertie isn't the Chief because he's been around the longest. He's very good at interrogating suspects. After some subtle prodding and then some not-so-subtle threats, Adams sang. Adams admitted he was at George Burnhams' house at 3 Stock Avenue on December seventh. Further, he admitted that when he came out of the house, Hugh confronted him and they had a huge row in the middle of the street. You'll never guess who he was meeting."

"Was it a woman?" I asked. "A man?"

"It was Daniel Grey," McKay told me.

I paused and thought. "I've heard that name before. Where have I heard that name?"

"He's the leader of the Toronto branch of the National Unity Party."

"The Nazi group? But I thought all of the leaders of fascist and Nazi groups were interred at the start of the war."

"He wasn't appointed leader until late '41 after which he was held at the Petawawa military base for the entirety of the war. In December of '40 he was just a mouthpiece."

"Lipowicz was right," I said.

"No, according to Lawrence Adams, he simply received an invitation from his boss and, wanting to be a good employee and part of the group, he went along," McKay said sarcastically.

"He went along? That's his story? He just went along to get along, is that it?" I slammed my drink down angrily on the table beside my chair. "How many Germans, Frenchmen, Belgians, Italians did you meet during the war who said 'I was just going along' or 'I was just following orders' or 'I'm not in charge. This isn't my fault'. How many of those men did you arrest? How many of those men did you see hanged?"

"Too many," McKay said.

"Evidently, Adams senior thinks that this is the event that caused Hugh to disappear and enlist," I said.

McKay nodded. "The row in the street was so heated that Adams senior was worried that Hugh might turn over the names of everyone who was at Burnhams' house to the police. After that, Hugh was different. He hated everything his father stood for, everything he valued and he made no bones about it, either. They barely spoke after that day."

"Do you blame Hugh?" I took a sip of my drink and shook my head. "I suppose Adams didn't tell you this when you opened the investigation because he was worried you'd report him to the authorities?"

"He was worried that his reputation as a lawyer and that of the law firm would suffer. He also didn't want his wife or daughter to know. He was afraid if word got out they'd become social pariahs."

"Yes. It's bad for business when you're labelled a Nazi sympathizer," I said bitterly.

"The Chief has decided that the most likely scenario is that Hugh left town of his own free will. Whether he joined up using another name or just walked away from his old life to start a new one somewhere, doesn't matter. There's no evidence that any crime has been committed and Bertie doesn't think it merits any further investigation. It's not illegal for an adult to disappear and start a new life."

"What about you? Do you think this case merits further investigation?" I asked. "This new information casts Adams senior in a new light. He might very well have done away with his own son to keep him quiet."

McKay nodded slowly. "It's rather far-fetched but possible, I suppose. But at this point, there isn't enough evidence for an investigation to lead anywhere. There's no body, nothing to indicate Hugh Adams is dead. In fact, the postcards indicate just the opposite. The O'Halleran Bay Police Force has done all it can do."

A few weeks later I heard that Dorothy Adams placed advertisements in several major newspapers across Canada appealing for information about her brother. I thought she was making a terrible mistake and opening the door to all kinds of crackpots and flim-flam men but it wasn't any of my business. Still, I couldn't help but be bothered by questions. Why send the postcards? Why did Hugh wait seven months after the confrontation with his father to leave? And why did he leave in the early hours of the morning during his vacation in O'Halleran Bay? Wouldn't it have been easier to slip away when he was alone in Toronto?

Nine

The Tuesday after Dominion Day I was nursing a terrible hangover and I was in an absolutely foul mood when I dragged myself into work that morning. To make matters worse, the heat that started in May continued in full force through June and into the beginning of July and this was in the days before air conditioning. Wagner's fan at the front desk blew hot puffs of air around the room and only succeeded in irritating everyone. McKay, who had been stuck inside the station that morning and subjected to my crabby back talk, offered to buy me lunch at Hudson's when I was done work at noon.

"I don't know why you do this to yourself," McKay said, sliding into a booth at Hudson's.

"I never mean to," I said. I took the bench facing him and put my head down on the cool surface of the melamine table. "Halfway through a party, everything gets a little out of control."

"I wanted to ask you something. You know, away from the office so Wagner and Boucher couldn't hear," McKay started.

I lifted my head from the table slowly. "Oh, dear God."

A waitress hurried past, leaving two glasses of water on the table before moving on to the next customer.

"It's nothing like that," McKay smiled. "Hank Cardiff stopped by my house yesterday and invited you and me to dinner on Saturday night."

"Me?" I snorted. "Why me? Haven't I suffered enough?"

McKay reddened slightly. "He thought you were my girl." Seeing my expression, he shook his head. "Don't worry, I set him straight but he wants you to come anyway. He's worried that Ellen's new around town and hasn't made many friends yet. She spends a lot of time with his mother and the ladies at the church group. He thinks it would be nice for her to meet another woman her own age. You know, someone to exchange recipes with or to meet for tea or to partner with for cards. I told him we'd be along about four o'clock."

"I have no interest in exchanging recipes or playing cards with Ellen Cardiff," I told him.

"Oh, c'mon. It's just a little dinner. You're new here too. It might be good for both of you."

"Ellen doesn't have any friends because she's a judgemental prig and she's not likely to ever have any. You've met her. She's horrible."

The waitress returned and McKay ordered two sandwiches and a bowl of soup. I asked for water and plain toast.

"She's in my mother's church group," McKay hesitated.

"Ellen?" I asked.

He nodded and paused for a few seconds before continuing. "Ellen was talking to my mother at one of their meetings and told her that her parents died when she was very young and she was taken in by an elderly great-aunt from Hamilton."

I snorted. "Let me guess. The aunt is dead."

"Died when she was eighteen."

"I'm not surprised. Barbara Gagliacco told us that Ellen's father was a drinker and the family was poor. Ellen strikes me as the type of woman who would be embarrassed about that. She probably tells everyone she's an orphan so they don't find out the truth."

McKay sat back and reached for his glass. He looked past me and the glass stopped at his lips. A pretty blonde had just entered the restaurant. The man with her placed a proprietary hand on the small of her back and they made their way in our direction to a free booth near the window. Looking up, she saw McKay and smiled a polite but uncomfortable smile. She hesitated slightly but stopped in front of our booth.

"Joe. It's good to see you." Her voice was breathy like Ava Gardner and she looked like a cross between Grace Kelly and Ingrid Bergman. Beside her, I looked like a B movie actress used to playing washerwomen and housekeepers. I hated her instantly.

"It's good to see you, Claire," McKay said, genuinely. "And you too, Walt. I hope you're well."

"We're fine," Walt answered. "I don't think we've seen you since you got back. Hard to believe in a town this size." Walt laughed. It was a loud braying guffaw, like a donkey.

"Chief Parsons has me working odd hours," McKay answered.

"Say, you still got that old jalopy? I'm over at Campbell Motors now. We've got a pile of nice new cars just in. The war's over and new car production is booming. I'm authorized to take a hundred dollars off the top for any man who served," Walt said earnestly.

"I got rid of that old Ford when I went overseas. I'm driving a motorcycle now but come winter I'll keep you in mind," McKay told him.

"Winter?" I laughed. "You'll be lucky if that thing makes it to next week."

Claire had been watching me since they approached the table. Now she stuck out her hand. "I'm Claire Cook."

"Arvilla Badger," I said, taking her hand.

"Miss Badger is doing some secretarial work at the police station," McKay explained.

"It's temporary but it keeps me busy," I said.

A moment of silence stretched out amongst us.

Finally, Walt spoke up. "Darling, we should get to that booth before someone takes it."

"Yes, we should," Claire agreed automatically. "It was nice to meet you, Miss Badger, and to see you, Joe."

"Take care, Claire," McKay said.

The couple hurried off to their booth and McKay stared down at his glass of water.

"Let me guess. Claire is the girl who sent you the Dear John letter," I said.

129

"That's her," he nodded.

"She's very pretty and she seems quite nice. He's a bit of a knucklehead, isn't he?"

McKay smiled. "Walt's okay. He's a decent guy."

"It's worse when they're decent. Trust me, I know," I smiled ruefully. "If he were a real crumb you'd feel much better about the situation, completely justified in your anger. When they're like Walt it just feels like kicking a puppy. You feel like a monster."

"We weren't engaged. We didn't make any promises to each other." McKay sounded like he was trying hard to convince himself.

"If it makes you feel any better she probably hates his laugh."

The waitress arrived and set down our plates. McKay unwrapped his napkin and put it on his lap. "It doesn't."

Ten

July's heat brought terrible storms almost every afternoon like clockwork. The rain fell in a wall of water, hissing as it hit hot pavement and roof shingles and then evaporating into steam, creating a slightly demonic and hellish look to the whole town. Some nights it was perfectly still and clear but on other nights the rain started up again, continuing well into the middle of the night. Inside the cottage, everything felt damp, from the chesterfield and the newspaper to the bedsheets and my clothes.

"I can't believe I let you talk me into this. I'd rather be captured by the Nazis than go to this dinner," I told McKay when he opened the door of the Ford and got in on the passenger side.

"I couldn't say no. Hank and I were friends in high school and he wants to give Ellen a chance to make new friends. Plus, I bet they've got an electric fan," McKay said.

We pulled up to the Cardiff house on Champlain Street and I reached into the backseat for a cookie tin.

"Did you make cookies?" McKay asked, incredulous.

I gave him a disapproving stare. "Is that so hard to believe? I spent many hours learning how to sew, darn socks, stitch samplers, bake, cook, set a table, address dinner invitations and even grow a garden, thanks to Mrs. Schmidt and my father. I spent an entire year of Saturdays attending etiquette lessons from the horrible Miss Perkins in the basement of the church. I know enough not to arrive at a house empty-handed."

"Calm down. No need to flip your wig. You just seem to defy convention so I'm surprised about the cookies, that's all."

"I don't defy convention," I argued. "I just came to realize that most of the rules and limitations we spend so much time learning and defending and following so rigidly don't really matter."

McKay smiled. "I wish I could believe that, Miss Badger, but if the war taught me anything it was that we must ardently defend and uphold the rules and limitations."

We walked silently up the front cement walkway to the door. Ellen opened the front door before we could knock.

"Good evening Mr. McKay, Miss Badger," she said.

"Call me Joe," McKay said, handing his hat to her outstretched hand.

"And I'm Arvilla," I said.

"Please, leave your gloves and handbag on the table." She gestured to a wooden half-moon table sitting in the hallway. "I'm pleased you could come. You'll have to forgive me for inviting you with only four days' notice."

"Four days was more than enough time. Thank you for the invitation," McKay said.

"Dear, Joe and Miss Badger are here," Ellen called up the stairs.

"Please, you must call me Arvilla," I reminded her.

Hank hurried down the stairs, pulling on his shirt cuff and buttoning it.

"Where's your dinner jacket?" Ellen asked him.

"It's a hundred degrees out. Besides, I don't think there's any need to be that formal, Ellen," Hank answered.

"They call it a dinner jacket for a reason." Ellen pursed her lips and eyed him so coldly I thought for a moment Hank might turn around and run right back up the stairs to retrieve the jacket but instead, he reached past her and shook McKay's hand.

"Let's go into the living room. Ellen's made some lemonade," Hank said.

As we had done before, McKay and I sat side by side on the chesterfield. Hank made a move towards the pitcher of lemonade that was on the coffee table beside four glasses but Ellen quickly shooed him away.

"Darling, sit down. This is your day off. I'll pour," she said as she ushered him over to one of the blue wingback chairs.

"Arvilla, do you think you'll make O'Halleran Bay your permanent home?" Hank asked.

"I'm not sure what my plans are," I answered truthfully. "I'm working at the police station until the end of the summer and then I'm not sure what I'll do."

"With your qualifications, I'm sure you'd be a welcome addition to any typing pool," McKay smiled.

"I think I've had quite enough of the typing pool," I told McKay. I turned to my hosts. "I was a stenographer at army headquarters in London during the war."

"That must have been fascinating work," Hank remarked.

"Sometimes," I replied.

Ellen passed me a glass of lemonade and I set it down on the table beside me.

"Please excuse me for a minute," Ellen said, quietly slipping out of the living room.

"Were you overseas as well?" I asked Hank.

He nodded. "Army. I was an officer."

"You must have attended officer training in Brockville, then?" I asked.

"Yes."

"I had several school friends who would have been there in the summer or fall of 1941," I lied.

"I was there at that time. What a coincidence. I probably know them. What are their names?"

"George Anderson and Cecil Smith," I said quickly. I was quite a good liar when I had to be.

"Well, how about that!" Hank slapped his thigh. "You know old Cec? What a cutup! Cec used to make us laugh. The things he used to pull. I haven't seen him in years. Did he make it home okay?"

"Honestly, I'm not sure. I've largely lost track of that group of friends," I said.

Ellen reappeared in the living room with a tray of deviled eggs, which she set down on the coffee table with a little pile of dainty linen napkins.

"Ellen, Arvilla knows one of the fellows that was in officer training with me," Hank told her.

"That's lovely," Ellen answered automatically.

I pretended to search my memory. "You know who else would have been in officer training with you?" I turned to McKay. "The man whose disappearance you were investigating. What was his name? You were friends with him, Ellen."

"Hugh Adams," McKay answered.

Ellen made a face. "I was not friends with Hugh Adams. I didn't know him that well at all. I was friends with Barbara."

"Yes, that's him. Hugh Adams. Do you remember him?" I asked Hank.

"Let's stop all of this talk about the war," Ellen said abruptly. She smiled at her husband. "It brings back such unpleasant memories. I worried every day that you were gone."

"When I spoke with Barbara, she said you two met here in O'Halleran Bay," I said.

"We met at a dance at the Cedar Lake Lodge," Hank said. "She was the prettiest girl there and I had to dance with her."

Ellen looked at her husband fondly. "I knew from the moment he asked me to dance that Hank was a proper gentleman. That's why I didn't hesitate when he offered to drive me home after the dance was done."

"What can I say? I didn't want the night to end," Hank laughed.

"I think it's wonderful that you were able to keep in touch, even after Ellen went back to Toronto," I said.

"I think God or Fate had a hand in it." Hank smiled and looked adoringly at his wife.

"What do you mean?" I asked.

Hank sat back in his chair, assuming the posture of someone who was getting ready to tell a particularly good story. "I did my basic training in Toronto and during that time I had one night," he held up a finger and repeated for emphasis, "one night of leave the whole time I was there. On that night I went to the Beaver Club."

"The Beaver Club," I repeated, biting my lip.

"It was over on Dundas. It was a canteen run by the United Church Ladies Auxiliary. They had dances and a band on Saturday nights. You never went when you were in the service?"

I could just imagine the snickering from every male member of the congregation when one of the women from the church auxiliary stood up at the end of the Sunday service and announced that everyone should go down to the Beaver Club on Saturday night.

"No, I never went to the Beaver Club," I smiled slyly. "But I think McKay was a regular member, weren't you, McKay?"

"You met up at the Beaver Club?" McKay said, changing the subject and giving me a glance that told me to behave myself.

"It was the darndest thing. I had one Saturday night of leave, walked into the club and there was Ellen," Hank said.

"It was definitely fate," Ellen smiled adoringly, patting her husband's hand.

Fate my fat ass. If I had to put money on it, I would guess that Ellen had staked the place out the entire time Hank was in Toronto so she could run into him accidentally on purpose.

"She couldn't get enough of me," Hank joked. "Before I left for Brockville she sent me a stack of pre-addressed, stamped cards."

"I wanted to make sure you could keep in touch with your family and me," Ellen said.

"I had a big stack of the sappiest cards you've ever seen. I used to get a good ribbing from the boys about that."

I glanced over at McKay. We locked eyes. Silence fell over the room, as it often does with a group of people who don't know each other very well. I sipped my drink.

Finally, McKay spoke. "How long have you been married?"

"Thirteen months," Ellen said proudly.

"That's lovely," I said.

"We got married a week after I came home," Hank said. "Though, the honeymoon wasn't much fun. I was discharged after getting shot in the rear end."

"Henry Cardiff!" Ellen said sharply.

"It took me almost six months before I could sit for more than a few minutes," he added.

"That is quite enough," Ellen told him. "There's no need to talk like that in front of company."

"It's alright. I'm not offended," I laughed. "I was a married woman for a while."

Ellen looked at me. "Was your husband killed in action?"

"No, but if I'd stayed with him any longer I may have killed him," I told her.

She looked at me disapprovingly. "All marriages call for compromise."

I wanted to reply with something saucy and slightly off-colour but instead, I held my tongue and changed the subject. "Did you get married here in O'Halleran Bay?"

"Yes, I wanted to have a proper church wedding with all of Hank's family and friends. I knew it would break his mother's heart if he got married by the army chaplain in an office somewhere," Ellen said.

"I'm sure your family wanted to be there as well," I said.

"My parents have both passed on and I'm an only child," Ellen said sadly. "Hank is my family now."

"I'm sorry. My mistake. I was sure Barbara Fisher said that you have twelve brothers and sisters," I said.

Ellen snorted. "There's your problem, Miss Badger. You really can't put much stock into anything Barbara says."

"I must have misunderstood," I smiled.

"Barbara Fisher," Hank said slowly. "That's the girl who came to O'Halleran Bay with you, isn't it? The girl who took our picture?"

"Yes, darling," Ellen answered.

"Now that I think of it, Arvilla, it was taken on your lawn." Hank stood up and left the living room, turning left and disappearing down a hallway. He returned a few seconds later carrying a heavy frame. "Barbara took this picture on our second date."

I took hold of the frame and examined the black-and-white photo carefully. It was a beautiful photo, though I don't pretend to know much about photography, or art for that matter. Barbara had taken the photograph just at the right time of day and found the perfect angle to prevent shadows from creating darkened areas and strange out-of-focus objects in the background. Hank and Ellen were sitting on a blanket on the grass, he with his legs stretched out in front of him and his arms at his sides and her with her legs curled up under her and one hand on his upper arm. Behind them, in the background, my father's tin boat was propped up against the shed, along with two oars, the base from a cement bird bath, a large metal steamer trunk, a metal bucket and several croquet mallets.

"I haven't seen that boat in ages," I said, pointing to the background. "It must still be in the shed."

"It was way in the back. Your father came over early that morning and dragged it out of the shed for us. We rowed over to Pottery Island that day."

"It's a beautiful photograph, so detailed that you can even see the weave of the blanket you're sitting on," I said.

Hank turned to Ellen. "It was a gift from Barbara. It's a shame she couldn't come to the wedding. She's out west now, isn't she, Ellen? Calgary?"

"Yes. Unfortunately, we've lost touch." Ellen took the photograph from him. "Please excuse me while I put this away and check on supper."

I stood. "Allow me to help."

"No. You're a guest. A good hostess would never let a guest help in the kitchen."

"At least let me set the table," I offered. "We can leave the men alone to talk about the Beaver Club or whatever men talk about."

Ellen paused then nodded. "Certainly."

I followed Ellen into the kitchen. It was small, as was the fashion of kitchens at the time, but impeccably clean. Blue gingham curtains hung above the window under the sink. Matching towels, potholders and an apron hung on a set of hooks. "Where are the plates?"

She donned the apron and opened the oven door. "The cupboard next to the sink."

I opened the cupboard door and stared. All of the handles on the teacups faced the same way. The designs on eight water glasses and four juice glasses all lined up. "My goodness, your cupboards are so organized," I said.

"Thank you," Ellen said. "You were married. You know that it's a housewife's responsibility to create a home her husband can be proud of."

I grabbed four plates from the cupboard. "We didn't have much of a home, just a little flat with a few pieces of used furniture and two chipped coffee mugs. There wasn't even a stove for cooking, just a little burner that only worked half of the time."

"How long were you married?" Ellen asked.

"Two years." I opened the drawer closest to me and took out some silverware.

"May I give you some advice?" she asked, bending down and poking at the roast without looking at me.

"Sure," I answered hesitantly.

"O'Halleran Bay is a very small town and quite conservative. You don't want to give anyone the wrong impression. I wouldn't tell too many people about your past."

"My past? I'm divorced. I didn't work in a brothel," I said.

She lifted the black metal roasting pan from the oven to the stove and closed the oven door with her foot. "Suit yourself. I'll let the men know it's time to wash up if you'll finish setting the table."

I nodded and quickly finished setting the table. My eyes roamed around the combination kitchen and dining room and fell upon a stack of books neatly lined up on small shelves running the length of the cupboards on both sides of the window. In addition to several cookbooks, Ellen had a large collection of books about decorum; Emily Post's book "Etiquette", and Margery Wilson's "Pocket Book of Etiquette" (whoever she was). One, in particular, was hysterical. It was called "What a Young Wife Ought to Know".

"Smells great," Hank said, coming into the dining area.

"Thank you, darling," Ellen beamed. She placed a platter with roast beef, potatoes and carrots on the table and handed him a carving knife. "It's your mother's recipe so you must give her all the credit."

"It looks delicious," McKay told her.

We sat down and began passing the platter around the table.

"It's been a long time since I've had a meal like this," I said.

"Poor dear. It must be so dull and dreary having to eat supper all by yourself every night," Ellen said, sadly.

I'd be damned if Ellen godamn Cardiff was going to pity me. I smiled broadly. "Not to worry, Ellen, dear. When it gets dull and dreary, I just turn on the lights."

Hank laughed. "Arvilla, you are a cut up. Isn't she a cut up, Ellen?"

Ellen smiled a tight smile. "Quite."

Once the platter made its way around the table, I picked up my fork and began to eat.

"The roast is tough," Ellen said after her first bite of meat.

"I think it's very good," McKay told her.

She shook her head. "It's tough. I must have over-cooked it."

"It's just fine Ellen," Hank said.

"It's tough and flavourless," she told him.

She picked up her plate and scraped the meat back onto the serving platter. Then she did the same with mine, McKay's and Hank's. She took the meat on the platter, marched into the kitchen and dumped the entire roast into the garbage can. Calmly, she returned to her seat, picked up her napkin and smoothed it down onto her lap.

"I apologize," she said. "I simply don't serve my guests meals that are subpar. There are plenty of potatoes and carrots. I promise you won't go away hungry."

I've often wondered if, at that moment, Hank Cardiff realized that there was something truly wrong with his wife. I can still see the look on his face. It was a mixture between incredulity and embarrassment. McKay and I couldn't eat and get out of there fast enough.

"She's bananas," I told him once we finally managed to escape to the car. "Is this what happens to men when they're faced with the prospect of dying in a war? They just attach themselves to the first girl who comes along?"

"Not normally. I don't know what Hank was thinking."

I put the car in reverse and slowly backed out of the driveway. "I'm positive she's the one who sent the postcards. Hank was at officer's training in Brockville about the same time as Mrs. Adams received the postcards and Ellen sent Jack the same type of cloying cards Mrs. Adams received."

"I just can't imagine that Hank would willingly send postcards to Mrs. Adams. His choice of wife might be questionable but his morals never were," McKay said.

I thought for a moment. "The postcards are the one aspect of this case that never made any sense. If Hugh Adams really did send them, there would have to be a record of his enlistment."

"Unless he enlisted under another name," McKay reminded me.

"But only officers were trained in Brockville. To be an officer, you must at least have proof of a high school diploma."

"He may have used someone else's papers. It wouldn't be difficult."

"Hank knew him, even if only in passing. Surely he would have recognized him and wondered why he was enlisted under another name."

"By the way, how did you know Cecil Smith was there at the same time as Hank?"

"I didn't. I don't know Cecil Smith. Or George Anderson. Cecil and George are popular first names. Smith and Anderson are popular last names. I took a chance," I told McKay. "Look, it stands to reason that if Hugh Adams didn't send the postcards himself then whoever sent them wanted to keep up the pretense that Hugh was alive and had enlisted. Therefore, whoever sent them must have already known that Hugh was dead."

"We've already been over this. Ellen could not have possibly overpowered a hundred-and-eighty-pound man, killed him and then disposed of his body."

"No. But Hank Cardiff could have."

McKay laughed. "Oh, G'won! Now it's a conspiracy? Miss Badger, whatever you did in the war must have scrambled your brain."

"Hugh and Barbara arrive home," I began. "Hugh is drunk and angry. He's yelling. Barbara goes to bed. She was in the yellow room, the one I sleep in.

It's at the back of the house, the furthest part away from the water. Ellen tells Hugh to leave but he's angry. They argue and she gets him to go outside. He attacks her but Hank shows up. They fight and Hugh is hit over the head. Ellen and Hank panic and hide the body. As long as there is communication from Hugh, his parents think that he's still alive and never go searching for him."

"You've been watching too many moving pictures. Barbara never saw Hank at the cottage," McKay pointed out.

"Hank could have been in the front bedroom," I said.

McKay snorted. "I can almost guarantee that Hank was not in the front bedroom that night."

"What about Pottery Island? The day that Barbara took the photograph, Hank said they took my father's boat and rowed over to Pottery Island. Could Ellen have put Adams' body in the boat and disposed of it on Pottery Island?"

McKay considered the idea. "I never thought of that. It's less than two kilometres to the island from your cottage and Cedar Lake was calm the night Adams was last seen. Ellen certainly could have rowed to the island but she doesn't have the strength to get Adams in and out of the boat. Not to mention that people have regularly visited the island during the last five years. Someone would have seen a dead body."

"The beach area faces south. That's where visitors dock their boats and get out to picnic and swim. My cottage faces the west side of the island. Ellen could have rowed in a straight line from my cottage to the island then dragged Adams out of the boat and inland, just out of sight."

"The west side of the island is covered in large rocks. Ellen couldn't have moved a body by herself over rocks to get inland," McKay insisted.

"Then she had help," I countered.

McKay sighed. "I think Ellen's as bananas as you do but I don't think she had anything to do with Adams' disappearance. I know that Hank Cardiff certainly didn't." He paused. "But it's not a bad idea to take a look around Pottery Island. If Adams fell into the lake and drowned, it's possible that his body could have floated to the island and it could have become caught on the rocks. It's unlikely but the freezing and thawing of the ice the following winter and spring could, in theory, have separated and scattered the remains in between the rocks where they wouldn't be visible."

"I think the boat is still in the shed. It's Sunday tomorrow. We could row out there and take a look around. Wait a second. You're not just humouring me so you can see me in a bathing suit, are you?" I turned left on Arbuckle Street and then made a quick right onto Palmer Street. "It's number twelve, isn't it?"

McKay nodded and I pulled into the driveway of his parents' large three-storey brick home.

"How's ten o'clock?" I asked.

"Ten o'clock? In the morning? Can you be ready that early?" he teased.

"On a Sunday? Not usually but I can make an exception for you," I told him.

He smiled and opened the car door. "I'll see you at ten, Miss Badger."

Eleven

It was just after seven o'clock and still too early and too light outside to go to bed. I tried to read but gave up after a few minutes. The inside of the cottage was hot and damp, even with all of the windows open. In the months that I'd lived at the cottage, I hadn't even peered inside the shed and I decided that I had enough time before nightfall to make sure that the boat was indeed in the shed and in good enough condition for McKay and me to use it the next morning.

I changed into a threadbare blouse and an old pair of slacks. Even though it was unbearably hot, I found a pair of rubber boots that had belonged to my father and slipped them on, making sure my pants were tucked in tightly at the top. I suspected

151

the shed was full of mice and I had a terrible (and slightly irrational) fear of them running up my pant leg.

The shed sat on the piece of land that juts out into Cedar Lake on the north side of the property. It was surrounded by water on three sides with a clearance of fewer than two feet of land all the way around it. Originally a small barn for horses and wagons, my father began using it as a storage shed when cars replaced horses. After fifty years of being battered by the high winds rolling off Cedar Lake, not to mention the moisture from being so close to the lake, moss grew thick on the shed's weathered boards. The tin roof was intact but rusted and its side walls leaned to the left. Inside, I knew it was packed full to the rafters with discarded furniture, lawn tools, boating materials and everything else my father had collected over a period of thirty years.

The shed door was bolted with a padlock and I found the key hanging on a nail in the broom closet next to a coal oil lamp. I took the key and the lamp and I crossed the lawn to the shed. After several attempts to turn the key in the lock, the rusted padlock gave way and popped open. I stuck the padlock in the pocket of my slacks and pulled the door open. The smell of stagnant water, earth, diesel oil and rot wafted out. I took a step inside and bent over to pick up a clay pot that was lying on its side at my feet. It broke in my hands, scattering old, mouldy dirt all over my boots. I cursed loudly and threw the shards of broken pottery behind me onto the lawn.

I lit the lamp and held it up, peering into the dark nooks of the shed. I could just make out the shape of the rowboat's hull at the very back, stuck in between an old cookstove and several broken chairs. For the next half hour, I cleared a path to the boat, carrying out items and sorting them into three distinct piles: a garbage pile, a pile of metal that could be hauled away and reused and a pile for things I wanted to keep. By the time dusk started to move in, the only things I'd found worth keeping were a shovel and a boat oar. I had just made up my mind to quit when I saw my mother's old steamer trunk wedged between the front of the boat and the edge of the cookstove.

The metal and brass trunk had a slightly domed top and was three and a half feet tall standing on its end. Inside, five drawers lined the right half of the trunk and a wardrobe with hangers and a little ironing board filled the left side. My grandmother had purchased the trunk to take my mother on a trip to England, a trip my mother had never taken because she got pregnant with Johnny, ran away and married my father. I grasped the leather handle at the top of the trunk and was surprised that the wheels still spun easily, even on the hard-packed dirt floor. I tipped it on two wheels and pulled it backwards out of the shed, wheeling it onto the lawn before setting it down. The latch was rusted shut so I took a metal bar from the scrap pile, stuck it as far as I could under the latch and pried. The old latch gave way, then fell off onto the grass. I grabbed the handle and lifted the heavy lid.

During the war, I was ten feet away when they pulled a member of British Intelligence (and a dear friend of mine) out of the Thames where he'd been floating for about two weeks. It wasn't just the scent of decaying flesh that I'd smelled that day. No, that could be easily identified; that was the smell of a leg of lamb or a roast of beef that had been left out on the kitchen counter too long. There was something else, a smell that wasn't just the biological smell of a body and all of its organ systems breaking down. It was a cold and heavy odour, foul but slightly sweet and empty, like when air is removed from a space and a vacuum is created. This was the true smell of death and this was the smell that floated out of the trunk.

The same plaid Eaton's blanket that was in the picture Barbara Gagliacco had taken of Ellen and Hank lay crumpled inside, discoloured with streaks of blue-green mould and dried brown patches. My hand trembled slightly as I slowly reached forward and grasped the end of the blanket. I held my breath and pulled it back quickly.

The remains of a body lay haphazardly among the wooden hangers on the wardrobe side of the trunk. Snatches of light brown hair still clung to patches of flesh on its head. What remained of the skin looked like a wet paper bag wrapped around bones. There were no eyes in the eye sockets, no internal organs but perversely, the teeth shone white and straight in the mouth. Thick black fabric swathed parts of the body. Like many dead bodies I'd seen, the feet had become detached and the shoes, still full of foot bones, had been jostled when I moved the trunk. The right shoe lay in the middle of the trunk and the left shoe landed next to the right arm.

"You stupid, stupid, stupid woman," a voice hissed behind me.

I knew it was Ellen Cardiff even before I stood up slowly and turned around to face her. I tried to keep my voice neutral, as if I discovered dead bodies all the time, as if I didn't think that she was a killer. "I think we need to call Chief Parsons."

I made a move forward and she grabbed my upper arms.

"Ellen, we have to call the police," I said calmly.

"Why do people always ruin everything for me?" Ellen whispered angrily.

"No one wants to ruin anything for you, I promise. I think Hugh Adams is in that trunk and we need to call the police." I spoke calmly and slowly, playing stupid to try and diffuse the situation just like the C Int C trained me to do before setting me in von Baumann's path. I pulled my arms from her grasp.

"Shouldn't I have a chance at happiness? Don't I deserve that?" she said fiercely.

"Of course you do," I said.

"You want to ruin it!" Ellen screamed.

"No, I don't." I backed away and tried to run between her and the side of the shed. She cut me off.

"My whole life I've had to fight for anything I wanted. No one helped me. No one gave me anything. I did it all myself."

"Of course you did, Ellen," I agreed.

She picked up the shovel laying on the ground. "Don't patronize me."

"What happened to Hugh Adams, Ellen? What did you do to him?" I asked cautiously, backing away from her in infinitesimally small steps.

"Hank liked me and I could tell that if I just had a little time, I could help him see that he loved me. I could show him that I was a perfect woman; pure and good and self-sacrificing. That's what men want. I could tell that's what Hank wanted."

That's when I knew the reason Ellen had killed Hugh. It was so mundane, so anticlimactic that it was laughable. "That's why you killed Hugh, isn't it? He was going to tell Hank all about Ellen Hale from Corktown."

"Hugh was going to ruin it, just like he always did. He was going to tell Hank lies about me and then Hank wouldn't want me anymore."

"So you killed him?"

"He was laughing at me." Ellen took a step towards me. "He was so drunk he could barely stand upright, but he was laughing at me. When you're from a rich family, people with power, you can act however you like. You can spend your nights drinking and rutting like a pig and nobody cares. You can walk around all day, a hero, shouting "Death to Hitler" and then scurry around at night secretly supporting the Nazis and no one cares. But I was never going to get the stink of that slum off of me. If Hank found out about me, he'd use me just the way Hugh was using Barbara." Her voice had taken on a hysterical quality. "You're just like him, you know. You think you're brilliant, witty even, but you're just crass. Did you think I was too stupid, too much of a boor, to understand your sarcastic little comments about the Beaver Club? Did you think you could fawn all over my husband in front of me and I'd just take it? Am I just supposed to take it because you're an upper-class bitch?"

"I'm not interested in your husband, I assure you. I don't think I'm of a better class than you and I certainly don't think you're stupid. I think you're very clever because I still can't figure out how you managed to convince Hank to send the postcards to Mrs. Adams. You did that, didn't you?" She nodded and I went on. "You outsmarted everyone. How did you do it?"

"I glued the card shut and put the stamp on the front, on the side with the picture. I addressed it to myself on the back, just like a postcard."

"Once it was mailed to you, you steamed it open and cut off the back of the card where Hank had written to you. You addressed it and then dropped it in the mailbox," I finished.

"I paid a newspaper boy to do it," she corrected me.

"You're no dope, Ellen."

I bolted to the left, hoping to catch her by surprise and run past her. I almost made it but at the last second I saw a dark shape in my peripheral vision, followed by a thud made by the shovel as it glanced off my arm. Intense pain radiated down my right arm and I fell to my knees. I reached for my arm and screamed a low, guttural scream that left me gasping for air and almost sick to my stomach.

I forced myself to stand and ran away from Ellen, moving swiftly down the beach and then into the lake. I don't know why I ran into the lake; my only plan at that point was to get away and get help. I managed to get thigh-deep into the water before I felt a hard jerk on my hair and was pulled back under the water. I clawed at Ellen's hands and kicked, losing both of the heavy rubber boots in the process. My heels dug into the soft sand, and I bent my knees and pushed until I boosted myself out of the water just enough to draw a breath. Within seconds, she pushed me under again.

I was determined more than ever that I wasn't going to die on my own damn beach in front of my own damn house. If von Baumann hadn't managed to kill me, I certainly wasn't going to let Ellen godamn Cardiff do the job. I sank my heels once more into the soft sand and started pushing myself back towards the shore. My head popped up like a cork, just enough so I could grab a breath of air before Ellen pushed me under again. I tried again but Ellen had finally figured out what I was doing so she pushed harder on my shoulders. I wrapped my good arm around her heel and tugged her foot out from under her. It was a move Johnny had used on me more than once when we were children and play fighting. She fell backwards and I rolled onto my stomach and scrambled to my feet, breathing so hard the air stung my lungs. Ellen followed me, only a footstep behind.

The way to the road was clear and I ran. I was halfway across the lawn when I stumbled on the uneven ground near the flowerbed. Ellen stumbled too but she fell. My hand touched something cool and concrete. It was the bird bath. With all the strength I had left in my one good arm, I pushed as hard as I could and sent the large concrete top down on her. There was a dull clunk...and then nothing. I kept running, down the grassy strip along the side of the road in bare feet, my clothes clinging to me, trying to breathe in between the sobs, running for the nearest house with a telephone.

I still have that damn birdbath. Every spring I used to pull it out of the shed and set it up in the peony garden. Now that I'm as old as dirt I get one of

my grandchildren or the teenagers from the neighbourhood to set it up, which they do begrudging-
ly because they're taught to be nice to little old
ladies. McKay mentioned once that maybe it was
bad form, maybe I should get rid of it, but I told him
I like to look at it. Before you think I have a morbid
fascination with death, I should tell you that I didn't
kill Ellen Cardiff. The top of the concrete birdbath
simply knocked her out for a while.

By the time Chief Parsons, Wagner, McKay and
Boucher arrived at Mr. and Mrs. Robinson's house,
I was sitting on the chesterfield, sipping tea and
shivering under a blanket. Boucher and Wagner
found Ellen walking down the road in a daze, blood
running down her face from a large gash on her
skull. She claimed she didn't remember trying to
drown me or killing Hugh Adams but I was never
entirely sure if that was just an act. Ellen was nothing if not clever. The Crown decided not to seek
the death penalty. I'm sure that was partly because
Canada always was loath to hang women and partly out of deference to Hank Cardiff, who walked
around for months in a stupor, looking like he'd
caught shrapnel in the head. Ellen was sentenced to
spend the rest of her life in a secure hospital ward.
I assume she's dead by now; most people from that

time are long dead and buried. Except me. I'm still here.

I wasn't much worse for wear, despite taking a shovel to the arm. I spent two weeks in the hospital in traction then another eight weeks in a cast. My arm healed up nicely, though it's slightly shorter than the left one and aches to warn me when a bad rainstorm is coming.

If I've painted myself as a hero in this little story, I don't apologize. It *is* my story after all and it makes me feel good to remember a time when I wasn't a doddering antique who holds up the checkout line by counting out the exact change for her purchases. But don't mistake my vanity for lies. Everything I've told you is true and happened exactly the way I've described it.

Stories, I've learned, are like Russian nesting dolls; the first story leads to another one, which leads to another and so on and so on. Each subsequent story becomes smaller but infinitely more complex.

Secrets are like that too.

My only hope is that I finish telling all of my secrets before this world finishes with me.

Thank you for your support!

As an independent author, I rely on reviews to attract more readers and to spread the news about my novels. If you enjoyed this novel, please leave an honest review on Goodreads or Amazon. Reviews don't have to be lengthy or fancy. You can just write "I liked it."

If you enjoyed Arvilla Badger's first mystery, join her and McKay in solving their next case, *Love in O'Halleran Bay*, coming soon.

Manufactured by Amazon.ca
Bolton, ON